Heartbreak Beach

A Novella
Bailey Thomas

Bailey Thomas Books, LLC

One person's perception is another person's reality.

Contents

Episode 1: Castaways

ELISE

"I can't wait to see how we work out in the real world," I passionately expressed while staring into Jared's eyes.

The ocean breeze was flowing through my hair, and I could almost taste the salt as we stood right by the water. Seagulls were squawking in the distance, and the warm sand was creeping inside my sandals. The sun's rays were caressing my skin, and the sounds of waves crashing echoed throughout.

"Cut!" the producer exclaimed from his chair. "I don't like it. It's not believable enough."

He stood up and walked over to Jared and me. The producer put his hand on my lower back and gently gestured me forward, so that I was standing even closer to Jared. "Can you say it again, but with more passion? Say it like you really mean it."

"I've already said it like a million times," I snapped back, rolling my eyes.

This was supposed to be an intimate moment between Jared and I, but every time someone from the television crew made us redo a scene, it lost some of its magic. This had to have been my fourth or fifth take filming this scene, and I was tired of saying the same thing over and over again.

"Well, if I want you to, then you will do it a million and one times because that is what is in the contract that you signed," he said with a smug look on his face. "Now, say it again with more intensity." The producer retreated back to his chair so that we could continue on with the scene.

I had signed up for a reality television dating competition, not to be some producer's puppet. However, the contract, that I obviously did not read before agreeing to be on the show, clearly stated that I would *be an active participant to whatever extent is required, or be subject to legal action*. Therefore, I was left with two choices—be sued by the production company or agree to break Jared's heart.

I had made it to the finale of *Heartbreak Beach*, an unscripted series that followed one man's journey to find love. There were initially twenty women in the competition, but Jared Bradley had narrowed it down to only me. On the episode that had aired last week, he sent the only other girl home, and the finale was supposed to consist of me accepting his invitation to leave the beach with him. However, the producer thought a better storyline would be for me to dump Jared and force him to leave the show single. If that had been the deal from the start, I would have had no problem complying, but over the course of filming I had fallen in love with Jared and was not too happy to hear that I was now supposed to break his heart. Jared evidently had feelings for me as well, since he had kept me until the end. The season had been a rollercoaster of emotions for him, and I felt bad that all his tears would be for nothing as I was legally obligated to shut him down.

I cleared my throat, and for what seemed like the hundredth time, I repeated the line that I had been directed to say. "It's almost time for us to go back to the real world," I muttered to Jared, trying to follow the producer's order of adding even more passion, "and I can't wait to see how things go between us."

Nobody had interrupted me that time, so it was safe to assume that the crew was satisfied with my performance. I thought reality shows were supposed to be free from any outside input, but clearly that was not the case. The head producer, Brent Knox, had been a pain to work with from the start. He had his hand in every single dramatic incident that occurred throughout filming. Brent even pressured some of the girls into voluntarily leaving the show, despite their strong connection with Jared. All he cared about were ratings and deciding which girls would be the most entertaining to keep on the show. Brent even tried to get rid of me a few times, but Jared threatened to quit if I was kicked off *Heartbreak Beach*. He was still insistent on finding love and wasn't going to let some producer ruin that for him. Fortunately for me, Jared and I had built a strong connection from the start. It was pretty obvious that he was going to bring me all the way to the finale, which was probably why Brent wanted me gone—he thought I was too obvious of a choice. Jared had signed a contract with the same obligations as I had, but he was a key factor to the show. Although he was also legally obligated to follow production's orders, Brent was less likely to control Jared's actions as he didn't want to anger the star of his show. Jared brought the ratings, and Brent knew that. Therefore, in order to achieve the dramatic finale that Brent had been craving, he couldn't force Jared into something he didn't want to do, but he sure could do it to me.

"Speaking of the real world," Jared began, redirecting my focus from the horrible decision I had at hand to the beautiful sound of his voice, "there is something that I've been waiting all season to ask you."

There was no need for me to anticipate any interruptions from the crew after Jared spoke. They rarely made him redo anything. However, I was hoping that they would make us restart the entire scene again, as we were now at the part of the show where Jared was going to ask me to leave the beach with him, and I was under strict direction to decline.

Brent Knox had approached me in my trailer before we had begun filming for the day to notify me that I was going to be denying Jared's invitation to leave *Heartbreak Beach* with him. The ultimate goal of the show was to end up with Jared, so I profusely refused Brent's request. Of course, he happened to have my contract with him, in which he proudly read aloud the part where I had agreed to follow production's guidelines. He also decided that it was the perfect moment to remind me about the amazing legal team that they had on staff, and how fast they would prosecute me if I went against the agreement. I tried to fight him on it, even though I knew I had no other choice. Ultimately, our conversation ended with Brent getting his way and me crying about my obligation to break someone's heart on national television while being prohibited to talk about any of the details of our discussion with anyone else, especially Jared. I was crushed, but not as much as Jared would be when I would have to embarrass him in front of all the viewers. A new episode of *Heartbreak Beach* aired every week, therefore, Jared would only have a couple of days to mourn in peace before the dramatic finale reached thousands of television screens.

I had been dreading the filming of the final episode all day, but I couldn't avoid it any longer as Jared and I were on the beach, face to face, with cameras surrounding us. The sunset created a great background, an intentional move by the television crew, and we were both dressed in white garments. I had on a flowy beach dress, and Jared was wearing a button-down shirt with khaki shorts. We looked like the perfect couple, both wearing the same color scheme, but it was just another planned moment from production. They thought our tears would show up better on our clothes if we were wearing a light color. Throughout the entire season, every single moment had been calculated, including this one.

The part of the beach where we were standing was decorated with candles and roses in the sand. Jared was smiling, still holding onto my hands and staring lovingly into my eyes. The man who had stolen my heart over the past few weeks was about to experience the ugly side of reality television, all because I wasn't patient enough to read the show's agreement in its entirety before signing it.

"Elise Rosenberg," Jared started, as if he was beginning a proposal speech. "Although our time on the beach has been limited, my love for you has been endless. I knew from the moment that you entered the beach that you were the one for me. We started this journey together, and I want to end it together as well."

I never thought I could fall in love from a show, but Jared and I had been inseparable from the start. Everything about *Heartbreak Beach* felt fake. The producers curated staged moments, some of the initial contestants were actresses added to create drama, and our reactions were often unauthentic as it was most likely just a scene that we had already ran through several times before. We only gave genuine reactions on the first take, but of course, that one was never used. However, Jared's and my feelings were far from rehearsed. We had a genuine connection that was about to be abruptly ended. Brent had given me the responsibility to create reality television shock waves, and there was no coming back from that.

"I came on this show to find love, and I can say, without a doubt, that I found it with you. Elise ..." Jared got down on his knee for dramatic effect, "... will you leave *Heartbreak Beach* with me?"

Brent was staring at me intently, anticipating the jaw-dropping final episode that he had been dreaming of in his conniving head. The love between two people was about to be ruined because some producer wanted a more entertaining ending. I knew I had to say no, but I just couldn't. I didn't want to. Jared was the realest part of the entire competition, and I didn't want to punish him for putting his heart on the line on national television. Staring at Jared on his knee, pleading for me to leave the show with him was enough to create knots in my stomach. I should have read my contract more carefully.

"Can I, uh, actually take a five-minute break?" I asked the crew, needing to collect myself before delivering the worst news possible.

"Is everything okay?" Jared asked, standing back up.

"Yeah, everything is fine," I answered nervously. "I just need a moment."

I quickly scurried off set and headed in the direction of my trailer.

"Everybody, take five!" Brent called out in frustration, signaling to the crew that we would take a short break in filming. Brent needed to have control over everything and my sudden need for a breather was not on his agenda.

When I finally made it inside my trailer, I took full advantage of finally being alone for a moment. There was no such thing as privacy while filming a reality television show, so I needed to gather my thoughts quickly before a camera was shoved in my face. There was a lot on my mind. I had to make one of the biggest decisions of my life. There were more than just my feelings at stake. Ultimately, I had to choose whether to preserve Jared's heart or follow my contract. I needed a quick moment of silence to gather my thoughts before deciding. However, after less than a minute of being by myself, I heard a knock at my door.

"Elise, is everything okay?" I heard Jared call out from the other side. "Can I come in?"

Jared was the only one who I was willing to ruin my solitude for, so I quickly ran over and opened the door, hurrying him inside before anyone noticed that we were together. I was pretty sure there was another clause in my contract that prohibited me from being alone with him unless it was being recorded, but I wasn't one hundred percent sure as it was a large document that I had only skimmed. The opportunity to be on a show designed to find true love was all the incentive I needed to sign up.

"Elise, what is going on?" Jared asked in a panic when he was finally safely inside my trailer.

"Shh!" I whispered, covering his mouth with my hand. "We have to be quiet. He's going to come after me any minute now."

"Who? Who is going to come after you?" he questioned frantically, freeing himself from my hand that was shielding his mouth. "Elise, tell me what is going on."

I peeked outside of the window to ensure nobody was coming. I didn't see anyone, but I knew we only had a few minutes before we were going to be called back to set.

"I can't tell you," I explained. "Just know that I love you, and I always have."

"I love you, too," Jared proclaimed, inching toward me and tucking a loose strand of my hair behind my ear. "Whatever is on your mind, you can tell me," he explained. "I promise you that it won't make me love you any less."

I contemplated my options. Telling Jared what Brent and I had spoken about earlier was a breach in my agreement, but seeing the kindness in Jared's eyes as he was staring deeply into my soul made my love for him only grow stronger. I couldn't betray the man who had made me feel more seen than I had ever felt in my entire life, even after having my face on a show that was broadcast to millions of viewers.

"You are not going to believe this," I whispered, still periodically checking the windows of my trailer to ensure nobody was nearby. "Brent came to my trailer this morning and told me that I had to break your heart on the show. Believe me, I tried to fight him on it, but he wouldn't let me get out of it. I'm sorry, Jared, but he won't let me leave the beach with you."

"Wait, what?" Jared gasped, appalled by my recent revelation. "Why would Brent say that? Why would he do that to me? That doesn't make any sense."

"He doesn't care about you. He's never cared about you. It has always been about the ratings," I rapidly explained, clearly aware that we were running out of time.

Jared deserved to know what was going on behind the scenes. This whole show was a set up to cause emotional damage to the cast in order to please the public. We were all just pawns in a bigger game.

"That can't be right," Jared uttered in confusion. "We can't end the show like that. I love you, Elise. I'm leaving the beach with you whether Brent likes it or not."

"I love you, too, and I wish that was a possibility, but I signed a contract. We both signed a contract. There's nothing we can do." I was on the brink of tears, but knowing that Jared felt the same way about the situation as I did made me feel at least a little better.

Jared started pacing around my trailer, although there wasn't much room to work with. I thought he was going to get dizzy with all the circling he was doing, but eventually he lit up, seemingly full of hope that there was a solution to our major problem.

"I know a way out of this," Jared shared after contemplating the giant mess we were in. "My aunt is an entertainment lawyer. I can just call her and she will set everything straight."

"You are forgetting that Brent has our phones, IDs, and wallets stored in his trailer on the other side of the beach. Even if we were able to make it there without anyone noticing, there's no way we would be able to get inside. It's probably locked or something." I began to freak out as time was ticking and we were running out of options.

The entire cast had surrendered their personal belongings when we first started filming. The crew was concerned that we would leak sneak peaks of the show, so they prevented us from sharing any private content. Jared and I had nothing but the clothes on our backs, and that was not helpful in a situation like this.

"We don't need our stuff," Jared explained. "Let's just find a way to get to my aunt. Arizona isn't too far from California. I'm sure we could just hitch a ride or something."

"Hitch a ride? Are you crazy?" I questioned. "We can't just leave the set. Then, we would really be in trouble."

"Well, do you have a better idea?" Jared asked.

I wasn't even planning on escaping, so of course I didn't have a better idea, but anything sounded better than running away. It was only a matter of time before the crew noticed that the last two cast members were nowhere to be found.

"Two minutes!" I heard Brent call out in the distance, indicating that our break was more than halfway over.

"If we are going to leave, then we have to go now," Jared instructed. "Do you trust me?"

I knew it was an insane plan, but the entire time of filming consisted of nothing but curated drama. Every second of my day was carefully planned out and often times embellished in order to create drama and entertainment. Although agreeing to completely abandon the set of a show that was in the process of filming its final episode was a crazy idea, this was my chance to give Brent the plot twist that he truly never saw coming. This time, it was my turn to create shock waves.

"I trust you, Jared. Let's do this," I affirmed, motivated by finally seeing the downfall of producer Brent Knox.

Without any further hesitation, Jared grabbed my hand and quietly led me to the front of my trailer. He hesitantly opened the door, and we observed our surroundings before stepping outside. Most of the crew had returned to set by now, so there was no one around to notice us. Additionally, the sun was rapidly disappearing, giving us the shield of darkness. Brent was going to be enraged if the finale was not accompanied by a beautiful sunset, but he was going to be even more upset when he realized that his dream scene would not be happening.

"This way," Jared whispered, pulling my arm toward the direction of the lot where the crew parked their cars.

I tried to stay light on my feet as we raced toward the parking lot. I didn't want to trample against the ground and cause a bunch of noise, but it was difficult to keep up with Jared's pace. I was just as eager to get away as he was, but my legs weren't capable of moving as fast as his were. I could tell he was slowing down so that I wouldn't get left behind, and I felt bad that I was already holding up our journey before it had even started. I ran as fast as I could, trying my best to not slow us down.

I was only able to finally catch my breath when we eventually made it to the parking lot. As soon as we reached it, Jared began pulling on the handles of various car doors.

"Your plan is to steal a car?" I shouted as quietly as possible.

"We are not going to steal it. We are going to borrow it," Jared reasoned as he hopped from one car to the next. "Victoria, the hairstylist, leaves her vehicle unlocked with the keys hidden under the passenger seat."

"How do you know that?" I breathlessly asked, still trying to recover from the run.

"Because that's what hairstylists do," Jared answered confidently. "They gossip and say random details about themselves."

Jared had a point. I was pretty sure I knew more about Victoria than I did about myself. It was like it was impossible for her to do my hair unless she was talking at the same time.

"There's just one problem," Jared continued. "I don't know which one is hers."

Not being aware of which car belonged to Victoria definitely posed an issue, but Jared continued to methodically comb through the parking lot. He briefly pulled on the handle of each car, and once he realized it was locked, he immediately moved on to the next one. There were so many cars that the crew would probably come looking for us before we even found Victoria's, so I knew we had to figure out a different plan.

I scanned the lot, ignoring the cars that Jared had already checked, until my eyes landed on a vehicle that could only have belonged to our loud and obnoxious stylist.

"Jared," I said, catching his attention, "it has to be that one."

With the ounce of energy we had left, we raced toward the pink Mini Cooper, awkwardly parked next to a huge black SUV. Jared immediately tried the door handle, and it opened after a slight tug.

"Great work, detective," Jared noted with a sly wink.

Now wasn't the time to admire his charming personality, but if I had to escape the filming of a reality show in order to find an entertainment lawyer to avoid being sued by a production company, I was glad it was with Jared.

We hopped into the car, and just as Victoria had described, the keys were shoved under my seat. I frantically grabbed them and handed the keys to Jared.

"Let's get out of here," I uttered, once we had secured our mode of transportation.

Jared started the engine, but before he pulled out of the parking lot, he leaned over and gave me a kiss that had more feeling behind it than any of the other ones in the past.

"Thank you, Elise," he muttered.

"For what?" I questioned, caught off guard by the sudden gratitude.

"For not breaking my heart on national television," he explained.

I could've basked in that moment with Jared forever. I enjoyed every second I got to have with him without a camera being shoved in our faces, but I couldn't soak in the moment for too long as we were now on the run. Jared understood our dire situation, as well, and he abruptly drove off in a frenzy in the opposite direction of the set. We would probably have to stop and ask for directions eventually, but for now, there was only one road leading from the filming location, and Jared was speeding through it. I thought signing up for a dating competition was risky, but the real adventure had just begun.

2

Episode 2: Catch Us If You Can

JARED

I had always dreamed of stealing a car and racing it through the mean streets of the city. I just didn't think it would be because I was trying to flee a controlling producer, and I definitely didn't plan on my getaway car being a pink Mini Cooper. It was about a six-hour drive to Phoenix, but Victoria's car only had enough gas to last us about an hour at most. Elise was intensely staring out the window, checking the rearview mirror every few minutes or so to ensure we weren't being followed. Being on the run was more stressful than it was portrayed in the movies, but I would've definitely been a lot more afraid if Elise hadn't been by my side.

I didn't think I'd ever find the girl of my dreams on a dating competition show. In fact, I didn't even believe I'd be selected for the show in the first place. When I initially saw the commercial advertising for the casting call, I thought it was the most insane concept ever. Gathering a bunch of females on a beach to date a man that they had never met with the hope of falling in love and leaving the show together didn't even seem real. I applied, but more so as a joke. I had just turned twenty-eight, so it wasn't like I was desperate to find a woman, but it had to be every man's dream to be surrounded by beautiful women, all competing for your attention. Therefore, I sent in my audition tape without thinking I'd actually get selected. I figured they were looking for a guy who could double as a model. I wasn't bad-looking, but I didn't appear as though I belonged on a television screen, either. Everything about me was pretty average. I was around six-foot-one with dark hair and brown eyes. I had a slim build, but still possessed a bit of muscle. My dimples were probably the only features that were special about me. If someone had gone to their local grocery store, there would probably be about five men who looked exactly like me.

I was honestly surprised when the casting manager contacted me to continue on in the selection process. However, I was more caught off guard when a woman as stunning as Elise fell for me. She was way out of my league, which was why Brent had probably ordered her to dump me in the end. It was way too unbelievable that a girl like Elise would leave the beach with a guy like me. Her hair was a golden-orange color and it was so long, she could most likely sit on it. When it blew in the wind, it was like an explosion of fiery flames. Although her eyes were hazel, when the sun hit them just right, they almost appeared the same shade as her hair. Unlike me, she had many features that made her stand out. Elise was lightly dusted with freckles, her lips were of a peachy tone, and her smile was magazine-cover worthy. If she would've broken my heart in the finale without telling me the real reason why, I would have fully believed it was because she finally came to her senses and realized that she was way out of my league.

"Jared, are you okay?" Elise gently asked.

I was swerving off the road, and I had probably alarmed her with my chaotic driving. My thoughts were solely focused on reminiscing about how I had caught the attention of such a beautiful woman that I was drifting off the street. It had also been an extremely long night, and my adrenaline was starting to be replaced with the feeling of exhaustion.

"Yeah, I'm fine. Just a little tired," I admitted, correcting the car to prevent us from driving off the road.

"Do you want to switch drivers?" Elise kindly offered.

"I'm okay," I answered, "but we do need to find a gas station soon. I'm not sure how much further this pink Mini Cooper will go before it gives out on us."

I had been staring at the gas gauge for a while now, hoping it would magically stop going down, but it was clear that we wouldn't be able to drive for much longer without filling up.

"I saw a sign that said there was one a few miles away," Elise shared.

She had been staring outside the window the entire time, so I wasn't surprised that she noticed the sign.

"That solves one problem, but I think we have other things to worry about, too," I explained. "I'm sure Brent already has our faces plastered on every news station. We probably won't even be able to be seen in public without someone noticing us."

"We also don't have any money for gas," Elise added to the list of problems.

We should've left the filming location more prepared, but neither of us had planned on leaving so abruptly.

"Check inside the console and around the car," I instructed. "I'm sure Victoria has to have at least a few dollars shoved somewhere around here."

I slowed my driving to allow Elise to safely search around the car and climb in the backseat. The state of the car was honestly a perfect representation of Victoria's personality. Messy and chaotic were an understatement. Her car was filled with a bunch of useless junk. Old burger wrappers and broken combs were being thrown around as Elise tried to separate the trash from the salvageable items.

"Find anything useful?" I shouted to Elise in the backseat.

"Do you think we can do anything with shattered sunglasses and an old harmonica?" she proposed.

"Hm, probably start a jazz band?" I playfully suggested.

Elise giggled, and the sounds of her laughter sang in my ears. She was truly a living angel.

I continued to drive along the dark highway as things were being flung around the car. Eventually, the commotion coming from behind me ceased.

"Jared," Elise said with a hopeful tone, "remind me to thank Victoria later."

She climbed back into the front seat, first showing me a wad of cash that she had found.

"We hit the jackpot!" I exclaimed, even though it appeared to only be around a few hundred dollars. However, to us, it was worth a lot more than that.

"Oh, it gets even better," Elise stated, as the next items she pulled from the backseat were two wigs. I shouldn't have been surprised that a hairstylist had those in her car, but I genuinely wasn't expecting Elise's second successful find to consist of fake hair.

"I call the short purple one," I replied, followed by a slight chuckle. My only other option was a long, green wig that looked as though it should've been for a mermaid, but Elise needed it to fully cover her hair.

She put on the matted mess of green strands, and I wished I could've said that Elise looked absolutely ridiculous in it, but nothing in this world could have hindered her beauty. I thought the wig brought out her gorgeous features even more than before.

"How do I look?" Elise asked, owning the green mermaid look.

"Absolutely beautiful. It reminds me of when you first came onto the show. You showed up in a neon green bikini with a pink flower tucked behind your ear. Though, I will have to say that I prefer the swimsuit over the wig," I sarcastically let out.

"You remember what I was wearing?" Elise questioned.

"You're hard to forget," I casually noted, grabbing her hand and kissing the top of it.

Elise blushed, which made her look even cuter under the mangled wig. She placed the purple one on top of my head and adjusted it so that it sat perfectly.

"Am I stunning or what?" I uttered with my new purple mane.

"You look absolutely phenomenal," Elise teased.

"Well, thank you." I smiled, maintaining my focus on the road. "Don't forget to keep an eye out for that gas station."

She turned her attention back toward the window, but I made sure to carefully rest my hand on her thigh so she knew she was in good hands. I wanted Elise to know that she could trust me to lead her to safety.

My aunt was our lifeline to escaping this whole mess. I wasn't super close with her, as my dad never spoke that highly of his sister. My grandparents lived with us in our home in Boston, as they were too old to be on their own. I didn't believe my dad was too happy knowing that he was dedicating his resources to helping his parents while his sister had moved away to Arizona. She rarely visited, only going back to Massachusetts for major holidays, but when she did return, she and my dad barely spoke to each other. My aunt and I became a lot closer when I notified her that I was going to be on a reality television show. She had helped me negotiate my contract, which included loosening the reigns that production would have otherwise had on me. Brent didn't have the same control over me as he had over Elise. I wished I'd known Elise before filming so that my aunt would've been able to help with her contract, too, but it was too late. And now, all we could do was hope that my Aunt Laura would be able to work something out with Brent. We both had run off set, but I knew Elise was in a lot more legal trouble than I was because of the differences in how our agreements were negotiated.

"On the left," Elise pointed out her window, "there's a gas station."

I took a sharp turn off the main road when we approached the only establishment that we had seen since we had left the beach. There weren't any streetlights, so the glow of the gas station was very easy to see in the night. We were the only car in the lot, which was for the best, but it made the place seem more desolate. It was pretty run-down, and if it weren't for the figure of a cashier that I saw through the window, I would've assumed that it was abandoned. I pulled up to one of the pumps and put the vehicle in park.

"Stay in the car," I ordered Elise as I grabbed the wad of cash. "I'll be right back."

"No, I'm coming with you," she insisted.

I figured she would've been safer staying behind, but Elise had already gotten out of the car and was heading toward the entrance. I quickly caught up to her, just in time to hold the door open for her before she walked in. The chime of the door opening alerted the cashier of our presence. We tried not to appear suspicious as Elise and I walked up to the counter, but it was hard to act casual dressed in purple and green wigs.

"Can I get forty dollars on pump four?" I nonchalantly asked the cashier, handing her the money.

She took it and began pressing buttons on the register. The cashier didn't even say anything, or appear alarmed that two random strangers with bright colored hair had just walked in. She had to have been at least fifty years old, and she appeared to have smoked more cigarette packs than she had sold at the gas station. Her red lipstick was smeared, and her eye makeup almost reached her forehead. She probably looked more out of place than we did.

"Have a nice day," she responded with an attitude, handing me my receipt.

I was going to buy a candy bar as well, since I couldn't remember the last time either of us had eaten, but I didn't want to inconvenience the cashier any further. She seemed to already be irritated by our presence. We left the bitter woman alone and headed back to the car.

"She seemed lovely," Elise sarcastically remarked once we were outside.

"I can tell she really loves her job," I joked.

We strolled back to the pump where our pink getaway car was, with forty dollars less in my hands. I knew the cash wasn't going to last long and that we needed to be smart with how we spent it.

I began filling up Victoria's car with gas, admiring Elise's courage while I waited. I didn't think anyone else would have taken the leap of faith and agree to go on this journey with me, but she was something special. My love for her extended beyond what was shown on the television screen. Some feelings were just too intense to accurately portray on a reality dating show.

The gas pump clicked once the car had been filled and I calmly removed the nozzle from the vehicle and placed it back in its original position. Elise stood outside the car with me the entire time. We were both more concerned with the other person's safety than our own. I hopped back inside the Mini Cooper while Elise did the same, and I hit the road again with my partner in crime.

While I was driving, Elise still decided to focus most of her attention on the rearview mirror, constantly checking for other vehicles, but as the drive continued on, her eyes started to doze off. After about an hour, she had almost completely fallen asleep until she was awakened by the sound of her stomach growling. She quickly put her hand over it, as if that would stop the growling or hide the noise, but I could still hear it over the radio.

"Hungry?" I asked, wishing I had grabbed that candy bar for her.

"Maybe just a little," Elise bashfully revealed. "I don't want to slow us down, though."

"It's fine. I'm getting hungry and tired, anyway," I responded. "I think we have enough cash for a meal and a night in one of those motels." I looked around and noted the dilapidated town that we were driving through. It made the gas station look like a resort. I was more afraid of what was lying behind the motel doors than what Brent was planning to do to us, but we needed to sleep before we hit the road again. There was a burger joint at the end of the road, the only restaurant that appeared to be open, so I headed for it. As soon as I turned into the drive-thru lane, Elise's eyes widened. I could tell that this burger was about to be the highlight of her entire night.

"Don't worry," I started as I pulled out the wad of cash from my pocket, "dinner is on me."

Elise responded to my cheesy comment with a cute giggle. "Actually," she began, "dinner is on Victoria."

If Elise had found an engagement ring in the backseat of the car along with the wigs, money, and whatever else was hiding back there, I probably would have proposed to her in the line of the burger place. If I could travel across the west coast as fugitives with her, then I could easily see myself spending the rest of my life with her. I just hoped she felt the same way about me. *Heartbreak Beach* may have been a show curated for drama and filled with fake scenarios, but my feelings for Elise were very real. Not even a producer as evil as Brent Knox could ruin that.

3

Episode 3: Safe Haven

ELISE

Jared ordered us a burger, fries, and shake to share as we were trying to make the cash last as long as we possibly could. Spending a night in a motel was going to really put a dent in our funds, but neither of us would have been able to drive the rest of the way without getting the proper rest. There was so much clutter in Victoria's car that it wasn't feasible to sleep there either, so a motel was really our only other option. I wasn't thrilled with the amount of money that we would have left over to endure the rest of the trip with, but spending the night with Jared outweighed any of my concerns.

"You can have the last few fries," Jared offered, handing me the almost-empty pouch. We had decided to eat in the car, just in case someone inside would have recognized us, which meant our trash was probably just going to go in the backseat along with all the other garbage.

"No, it's okay," I countered. "I'm getting kind of full. You can have them." I handed the fries back to Jared, encouraging him to eat the few that were left. I was still starving, as the one meal wasn't enough to satisfy both of us, but I had noticed him letting me eat most of the food. He was hungry, too, but he was trying not to eat as much so that I could have most of it. Jared was selfless, but he needed his energy as much as I did.

"Thanks, Elise," he responded, devouring the fries within a few seconds. He wiped the excess salt and grease on his khaki shorts and took a sip of the drink. "Ready to stay in a five-star hotel?"

I laughed at his joke, but it was obvious that he was just trying to use humor to cover up the serious situation we were in. Brent Knox was a monster, and I knew he was going to utilize the full extent of the law to punish us as much as he could. He had it out for me more than Jared, which scared me even more. Brent's lawyers were probably going to make my life miserable through drawn-out legal battles, excessive monetary payouts, and irreversible damages to my reputation. Although neither me nor my family had the means to afford an attorney, the inability to work in television again would be the most detrimental part.

I had grown up in a low-income area of Ohio. My three siblings and I, and two half-siblings, lived in a two-bedroom apartment while being raised by a single mom. As the oldest, I was forced to grow up really fast and help her take care of my siblings while she was at work. Her job as a nurse wasn't enough to cover all the expenses, so I took up modeling at a young age to help bring in some extra income. At first, I just photographed for local newspapers, but apparently my red hair was appealing to a lot of magazine editors who quickly offered me jobs to shoot for covers. When I turned nineteen, I moved to Miami for better work opportunities and sent money back to my family in Ohio every other week. This arrangement had been going on for the past eight years, and though our financial situation wasn't as dire as it once was, my family still relied on my bi-weekly checks to help fund their lives. Therefore, Brent wasn't only going to ruin my livelihood, but my family's, as well. I knew he was going to make sure that I would never work in entertainment again, while drowning me in legal bills. I just really hoped Jared's aunt was a great lawyer, because I needed a miracle to get out of this.

While Jared was searching for the least sketchy motel to stay at, I snuck a few glances at him, admiring his internal and external beauty. He had such a kind heart and a handsome face to go with it. I hated the position we got ourselves in, and I regretted not reading my contract more thoroughly, but I didn't regret running away with him. Reality television, and the entertainment world in general, were full of fake people doing whatever it took to get to the top, even if it meant compromising their values. Jared, however, was the complete opposite of that. I could tell by the way he treated all the women on the show. Even if he was planning on sending them home that week, he still gave them his full effort and attention, and he never made anyone feel unwanted or unseen. Jared and I were a special couple, and Brent was trying to ruin that in the cruelest way possible.

"I think we found a winner," Jared exclaimed, turning into a motel that I personally would have never chosen to stay at. However, it appeared to be in the best condition compared to all the other buildings, which wasn't really saying much.

"I can't wait to finally lay my head down and take this wig off," I returned. "It's so itchy."

I vigorously scratched my head, almost pulling the entire wig off. I thought I looked like a mangled mess in the fake hair, but Jared actually pulled off purple really well.

Jared parked the car in a spot as far away from the main street as possible. I was glad that we were even further hidden by the darkness of the night, but when I got out of the car, I couldn't even see three feet in front of me. I could barely make out the outline of Jared, but I carefully walked around the car toward him, blindly reaching around until I felt his hand.

"Sorry," I exclaimed as my sudden tight grip alarmed him. "I can barely see anything."

"You don't have to apologize, Elise," Jared calmly relayed, interlocking his fingers with mine. "I'll never complain about the opportunity to be able to hold your hand."

I felt my face turn bright red, but it was too dark for Jared to notice. Even in the parking lot of a suspicious motel, he still had the ability to make me feel safe.

He confidently led me to the main building, carefully holding on to me the entire time. When we eventually made it inside, I was temporarily blinded by the lights as my eyes took a minute to adjust to the sudden brightness. After a few seconds of trying to regain my eyesight, I found myself even more unimpressed with the inside than I was with the outside. It was clear that the motel would not have come close to passing any type of inspection if it had to endure one.

"Hello, sir," Jared voiced to the receptionist who seemed surprised to have visitors. His bushy eyebrows furrowed at the sight of us. "Me and my wife would like a room for the night."

I was so busy counting all the roaches on the floor that I almost missed Jared's reference to me as his wife. I used my mangled wig to cover my blushed cheeks and cheery smile.

"One hundred dollars," the man casually informed Jared, typing away on his computer.

With how fast he responded, it almost seemed like a made-up number. In all honesty, the receptionist should have paid us a hundred dollars to stay at the dirty establishment. They probably hadn't had tenants in months. We were doing the motel a favor by even staying there.

Jared pulled out the wad of cash that was quickly dwindling and handed the correct amount over to the receptionist.

"Can I get a name for the room?" he responded.

"Um ..." Jared hesitated. "George?"

"Last name?" the receptionist asked.

"Uh ... um ... Washington?" Jared replied.

Good thing *Heartbreak Beach* was unscripted as Jared was a terrible actor.

"Can I get an ID Mr. Washington?" the receptionist questioned.

Jared already had a hard enough time coming up with a fake name. I couldn't imagine how long it would take him to think of an excuse for why he didn't have any identification on him.

"We actually left it at the restaurant in the previous town," I quickly interjected. "We called, and they claimed they couldn't find it, but I think the waitress stole it from us. I wanted to call the cops, but my husband said it wasn't worth the trouble." I held on to Jared's arm to further sell the fact that we were married. "On second thought, I actually think we should inform the police. Maybe we can have them meet us at this motel? I'm sure there is nothing about this place that would alarm the authorities if they arrived here."

I could tell that the receptionist was not too fond of the idea of having a police presence in the establishment by the way he stiffened up at the mention of them. He began frantically typing away on his computer before eventually handing us a key.

"Room 342," he announced.

"Thank you so much," I answered, taking the key card from him. I smiled at him before walking away, but he didn't return one back. I assumed he was just relieved to not have to deal with us anymore.

Jared held the door for me, and we went outside and up a few flights of stairs before eventually finding our room.

"You're a natural," Jared pointed out as I pressed the key card against the door.

"I've spent a lot of time around actors," I admitted, opening the door.

The door creaked opened and a rush of musty fumes hit my nose as soon as I walked into the room. Bugs scattered when I turned on the light. There was one queen sized bed in the middle with cream sheets on them. I believed they were once white, but now they were almost yellow with browning edges. The walls were stained from water damage, and the curtains covering the window were falling apart. There was a dresser with an outline of a television stand in the dust on top of it, but no television. It appeared as though there once was one, but it probably had been stolen. The only other pieces of furniture in the room were a rusty lamp and a torn up couch. I didn't even want to know what the bathroom looked like.

"I've seen worse," Jared optimistically announced, observing the worn out couch. "You can take the bed. I'll sleep on this."

Jared plopped down on the couch and a cloud of dust exploded from it. He tried to adjust himself on it and get comfortable, but the couch wasn't big enough for him. He would have had to sleep curled up in a ball in order to fit on it.

"Don't be ridiculous," I replied. "You are not spending the night on that thing. You can sleep in the bed with me."

"I just didn't want to assume anything," Jared cautiously explained.

"I know. It's okay," I said. "Trust me, I want you next to me tonight."

Jared smiled, seemingly relieved that I wasn't going to make him stay on the couch, but also relieved to know that I wanted him close to me. I knew Jared was just trying to be respectful of my boundaries, but he had been protecting me ever since I arrived at *Heartbreak Beach*. The least I could do was let him sleep in the bed with me.

"Do I even dare take a shower?" Jared questioned, walking toward the bathroom.

"I think you're better off rolling in mud," I answered, not trusting the quality of the water in the motel.

Jared took a courageous step into the bathroom. I didn't hear any screams, so it couldn't have been that bad, but he quickly returned with a few towels. They looked fairly untouched, so I assumed everyone else who had stayed in the room before us had also decided against showering. Jared laid the larger towels across the bed, covering the tainted sheets. He removed the moldy pillows and replaced them with the smaller towels, in which he crumpled up into balls.

"This should work for tonight," Jared relayed, staring at his recent work. "I know it's not what you had in mind, but hopefully this is good enough."

"It's perfect," I interrupted, just thankful for how thoughtful he was.

It was pretty late and we were both ready for the day to be over, so I adjusted the ripped curtains, covering as much of the window as I could, and turned off the lights before climbing into the makeshift bed with Jared.

"I don't know what's worse," Jared began when I was comfortably lying next to him, "sleeping in this disgusting motel, or when I had to send Sarah home on the first day of filming."

"Oh my gosh, do you remember how much she cried?" I uttered, recalling how devastated Sarah was to leave the beach. She clearly had signed up for the fame and not for love.

"I don't know why she was so surprised," Jared continued. "She told me that I wouldn't have been able to afford her lifestyle, anyway."

"She was on the show for the wrong reasons," I remarked.

Heartbreak Beach had initially begun with twenty women, but half of them were not on a journey to find love—they were on a journey to find a paycheck. The exposure that they would get from the show would land them a lot of job opportunities, so they wanted to last as long as they could, and get as much air time as possible. Unfortunately for them, Jared kicked them off before they could make a lasting impression.

"It's pretty easy to tell the real from the fake," Jared replied. "Reality television tries to portray this idea that everything is unscripted and unplanned, but I see right through that. I knew as soon as I met you that you were genuine, and the one who I wanted to end up with in the end."

"Really?" I questioned. "How could you tell? How did you know I was different?"

Jared started caressing my cheek and eventually started playing with my hair. I had ripped off the wig right when I walked inside the room, so this time he was touching my actual hair.

"I don't think even the best actress in the world could pretend to have even half the care in their heart that you do," Jared responded. "Brent can try to control you as much as he wants, but he's never going to be able to take away your authenticity."

Jared brought my forehead to his lips and gave me a gentle peck. He was somehow able to create a romantic and intimate moment in a run-down motel room.

"What do you think he's going to do to us?" I cautiously asked, afraid of the power that Brent possessed.

"I promise that whatever he tries to do, I'll be by your side every step of the way. You won't have to go through this alone," Jared revealed.

I let out a quiet yawn, not realizing how tired I was until I was finally feeling comfortable enough to let my guard down. Running away left me on edge, but being with Jared made me feel calm.

"Let's get some sleep," Jared encouraged. "We will head to my aunt's first thing in the morning. She will get this whole situation straightened out." He gave me another kiss on the forehead before eventually closing his eyes.

My body was exhausted, but my mind was running wild. I kept imagining what Brent would do the next time we saw him. I was curious if Jared's aunt would actually be able to help us, or if we would end up stuck in this awful situation until Brent eventually got everything he wanted. I tried to silence my thoughts so that I could sleep, but there was too much to think about.

"Jared," I whispered, before either of us fell asleep.

"Yes?" he replied, barely awake.

"Thank you," I said.

"For what?" Jared uttered.

"For not breaking my heart on national television," I shared.

Jared wrapped his arms around me and squeezed me in a tight cuddle.

"I was never going to send you home, Elise," Jared affirmed. "It was always going to be me and you in the end."

4

Episode 4: Star-Crossed Lovers

JARED

"Bernstein & Becker Law Firm. It's in Phoenix, Arizona."

I was trying to ask the receptionist for directions to my aunt's office. It was the same man from the night prior. He was surprisingly very eager to help us get to our destination, but it was probably because he wanted us off the premises as soon as possible since Elise had already threatened to call the cops on the motel once before. He handed me a map, along with written instructions on how to get there. The map was useless, as I didn't know how to read it, but the step-by-step driving directions were essential to our escape plan.

"Thanks," I responded, collecting the map and instructions. I gave Elise the map to hold on to, as she would probably have an easier time reading it than I would, and folded up the instructions to put inside my pocket.

"You've been a big help," I exclaimed.

"You're welcome, Mr. George Washington," he answered.

"Who?" I asked.

Although I was still a couple of years away from turning thirty, a few gray hairs had found their way onto my facial hair. I didn't think they were that noticeable, but considering the receptionist had just referred to me as one of the presidents who is often depicted with white hair, I started to rethink my entire appearance.

"That's your name, honey, remember?" Elise interrupted, reminding me that I had given the motel a fake name. "Sorry, it's been a long couple of days. Thank you for letting us stay at your ... uhh ... wonderful establishment."

Elise quickly directed me out the door, her green wig brushing against my skin.

"Thank you for the back up," I uttered, once we were out of earshot. "I forgot my cover story already."

"How could you forget?" Elise asked with a laugh. "You could've chosen any name, but you went with a U.S. president."

"It was the only name I could remember from history class," I answered, embarrassed by my lack of historical knowledge and inability to remember what I had told the receptionist yesterday.

I was never really good at lying, however, my older brother, Marshall, was a pro at it. Growing up, anytime something broke or was misplaced, he always blamed it on me, even if I had absolutely nothing to do with it. He was able to lie to my parents, straight to their faces, without any hesitation. I tried to follow in his footsteps, blaming my dad's shattered windshield on the neighbor instead of admitting that I had gone against his rules and played baseball in the front yard. I was only twelve years old. I wasn't even aiming for the car. I just remembered swinging my bat, and then hearing the sound of glass cracking. A boy my age lived next door, so when I ran inside to notify my parents of the damaged vehicle, I wasted no time in blaming it on Timmy next door. Unfortunately, my brother didn't tell me that when you lie, you have to make sure it's actually believable and that the person you blamed it on wasn't on a family vacation. My dad stormed over to Timmy's house, ready to make him pay for the damages he had supposedly caused, but quickly returned once he realized nobody was even home. I got my bat taken away and spent the rest of the week in my room. My dad eventually got his windshield fixed, but that was the last time I played baseball in the front yard, or lied to my parents.

"Maybe I should've just given the receptionist my real name," I admitted. "That way, I wouldn't forget it."

"Well, did you at least remember that I am your fake wife?" Elise asked, her eyes twinkling.

"Now that, I could never forget," I replied, leaning over and kissing her sweet lips.

Although I wasn't a fan of the situation we were in, it definitely brought Elise and I closer together. I was hoping that once everything was settled and my aunt was able to help us out, Elise would be the one who would have to remember a new name. I would love to make her Mrs. Bradley one day, and have her be my real wife. I was sure Brent had ruined a lot of reality television couples in the past, but he was in for a rude awakening with Elise and I. I didn't think even the most ruthless producer in the world could tear us apart. Everything about *Heartbreak Beach* was calculated and planned, but my love for Elise couldn't be scripted.

"Jared ..." Elise whispered, peering around me. "Look."

We had just left the lobby of the motel but hadn't made it to the car yet. I parked in the furthest spot I could find in order to not alarm anyone of our whereabouts. However, it was extremely difficult to hide a pink vehicle. Although I started to panic, I wasn't that surprised to see that there were two cops surrounding the car. We weren't concealed by the blanket of darkness anymore. The sun was shining, and the pink Mini Cooper was as clear as day.

"What do we do?" Elise questioned, holding on to my hand.

"Just follow me," I instructed as I led her back inside the motel.

We raced back into the lobby. Our good friend, the receptionist, was typing away on his computer. He didn't notice us at first, but when we approached the desk, he looked up. He didn't seem too excited to see us return so soon.

"Back again already?" he asked with an annoyed tone.

"Listen," I began, "we are kind of in a little bit of trouble and need your help."

I could tell Elise was starting to really freak out by the way she was squeezing my hand. I was also starting to panic, as I knew it was only a matter of time before the police started searching the motel and questioning the receptionist.

"Sorry, I can't give you a refund," he returned.

"We don't need our money back. We need transportation," I informed him.

He continued to type away on his computer, not as willing to offer his help as he was when I had initially asked him for directions earlier.

"This is a motel, sir, not a rental car agency," he responded.

I continued to grow in frustration, but the receptionist was our only hope.

"What's your name?" Elise politely asked him, diverting his attention away from me.

"Abraham," he returned nonchalantly.

"Wow, what a nice name," Elise complimented.

"It's a family name," he answered, appearing to lighten up a bit. "It's been passed down for generations."

"I love it. It's so powerful," she commented.

For the first time ever, Abraham actually smiled.

"My name is Rose," Elise explained, giving him a fake name. She was a lot smarter about it than I was, though. Rose was just a shortened version of her last name, Rosenberg, which was definitely a lot easier to remember.

"A beautiful name for a beautiful girl," Abraham noted, his smile widening.

"So, Abraham," I exclaimed, disrupting any further attempt of his to flirt with Elise. I wasn't usually the jealous type, but when it came to her, I was extremely protective. "How can we get out of here—fast?"

The sound of my voice appeared to wipe away the smile that he once had. I didn't think he was that motivated to help me out, but his budding crush on Elise seemed to make him more inclined to be of assistance.

"There's a bus station not too far away," he explained to me, although his eyes were still locked on Elise.

"Perfect, how can we get there?" I asked.

Elise yanked on my arm, almost pulling my shoulder out of its socket. Although it was rather painful, I probably would have been too focused on Abraham's answer to turn my attention to her if she hadn't tugged so hard.

"They're coming!" she squealed.

I looked out the window and saw two cops heading for the door. If we didn't act fast, any hope of getting to the bus station would be ruined, along with my chance of marrying Elise. If I didn't keep my promise of finding her a way out of this mess, she would never trust me again.

Before the police made it inside, I frantically pulled Elise around the receptionist's desk and crouched behind it. It was large enough to shield both of us, creating the perfect hiding spot.

"You're not allowed to be back here," he scolded.

"Please," Elise begged innocently. "We need you."

"We won't bother you ever again," I pleaded.

Abraham didn't have time to answer as I heard the front door fling open and the police officers walk inside. Their steps were slow, but heavy, and I could hear them getting closer.

"How can I help you?" Abraham asked in an unenthusiastic tone.

Elise and I knew he wasn't a fan of the authorities. Hopefully, he was bothered by them more than he was bothered by us.

"Excuse me, do you know who the driver of the pink vehicle parked outside is?" I heard a deep voice grumble. "That car was reported stolen yesterday."

"There's a pink car outside?" Abraham questioned.

"Yes, it is parked by the dumpster in the far corner of the lot," I heard the officer explain.

"Sorry, I have no idea," Abraham answered.

I could feel Elise's nervous body shaking against me. If it wasn't for the old air conditioning system that continuously made a rattling sound, the cops would've probably been able to hear Elise's heart thumping against her chest. She was still tightly holding on to me, refusing to let my hand go.

"Well, have you seen these two?" a female voice asked.

I presumed the officers had shown Abraham a picture of us. Although we were currently wearing colorful wigs, we were still recognizable. It would have been easy for us to be identified.

I could tell Abraham was contemplating his next answer as I saw him quickly glance down at Elise and I. I wanted to believe that he had our back, but we had already threatened to call the cops on him once. I wouldn't have been surprised if he wanted to return the favor and hand us over to the police.

"Yes, actually, I have seen them before," Abraham told them.

I began to sweat through my wig. I debated making a run for it, distracting them while Elise ran off to safety as it sounded like Abraham had chosen the police's side over ours.

"Do you know where they are?" the officer eagerly replied.

My heart sank and I heard a tiny gasp escape from Elise's mouth. To me, her charm was irresistible, but I guess Abraham was immune to it. I gently kissed her on the shoulder. It was an attempt to comfort her, but it was also potentially the last time I'd get to show her an act of love. I didn't know what was going to happen to us after today. We were not only in breach of our contract, but now we were car thieves. Our minor offense that may have just been punishable by a hefty fine and a ruined reputation had just increased to a crime that could result in jail time. As much as I hated the thought of being locked behind bars, not being by Elise's side scared me even more. I couldn't live with myself if she was arrested for something that was my idea. I shouldn't have encouraged her to run away from *Heartbreak Beach* with me. I should have just let her break my heart on television.

"I'm pretty sure they are headed for Daisy's Doughnuts," Abraham lied. "They asked me for directions there about twenty minutes ago."

"What were they wearing?" one of the cops inquired.

"I think they both had on dark-colored hoodies," Abraham described, which couldn't have been further from the truth. We both still had on our white outfits that we had been wearing from the final scene of the finale.

"We really appreciate your help," the female cop bellowed.

"Always here to help," Abraham returned cheerfully, although it was borderline sarcastic.

I breathed a sigh of relief, grateful that Abraham had decided to help out two strangers instead of the police. I patiently waited for the sound of the front door closing, so that Elise and I could get out of the motel as quickly as possible before they realized that the receptionist had lied. I listened to their steps get fainter and fainter, and I was waiting for the moment where we could pop up from behind the desk.

"Maybe one of us should wait here," one of the cops reasoned, "just in case they try to come back."

Sheer panic and fear filled my body again. There was no way we would be able to leave the motel unseen if one of them had decided to stay. My original idea of sprinting toward the door and causing a distraction while Elise went to safety had entered my mind again. I created this mess, and I didn't want to drag her down with me.

"You're more than welcome to wait here," Abraham quickly interjected, "but we recently had a bed bug infestation. They are everywhere—even in the lobby. We are still waiting to pass an inspection, and in the meantime, we are not accepting any tenants. In fact, it is advised that nobody even enter the premises until further notice, but again, you are more than welcome to wait here."

There was a pause in conversation, as the police were presumably contemplating whether they were going to stakeout in a bed bug infested motel or find a new place to hang out.

"On second thought, I'll just wait outside then," the cop ultimately decided.

"Suit yourself," Abraham replied.

The sound of footsteps returned until they reached the door. As soon as they left, I jumped up from behind the desk, pulling Elise with me.

"How do we get out of here?" I quickly fired at Abraham, who still rather have his sights set on Elise as he continued to refuse to look in my direction. I truly believed her overwhelming beauty was the only reason why Abraham decided to help us.

"There's a backdoor down the hall. Follow the road for about half a mile until you reach the bus station. Daisy's Doughnuts is in the opposite direction, but you won't have much time before the police come looking for you," he relayed.

I wanted to spend the next five minutes showing my appreciation for Abraham's kindness, but time did not allow for that. We needed to reach the bus station as soon as possible.

"Thank you so much," I briefly stated.

"Yeah, thanks for helping us out," Elise chimed in. "The story about the bed bugs was a good excuse to get the cops to leave."

Abraham simply stared back at her blankly.

"You were lying about the bed bugs ... right?" she followed up.

"Why would I lie about that?" he answered.

I quickly grabbed Elise's hand and pulled her down the hall toward the back exit. We didn't have time to lounge in the lobby, and we definitely didn't have time to discuss the status of the motel. At that point, tiny mites were the least of our worries. We only had a few minutes to find the bus station, grab a ticket, and head to Phoenix before the police realized we weren't at Daisy's.

We raced through the motel, toward the back door, and headed in the direction of our next destination.

It felt like Elise and I were Romeo and Juliet, two lovers overcoming the forces working against them. Or maybe, we resembled Bonnie and Clyde, a couple evading the police and always sticking by each other's side. Either way, I just hoped our love story had a better ending than theirs.

5

Episode 5: Head over Heels

ELISE

Jared and I made it to the bus station without any trouble. It was hard to run fast enough to make it there before the police realized we weren't at Daisy's Doughnuts, but slow enough to not raise any suspicions. Lucky for us, we were in California, so a couple wearing neon-colored wigs, dressed for a beach day, running through the streets of a small town, didn't catch the attention of too many people. Even the lady at the ticket counter didn't seem alarmed when we approached the window. She didn't give either of us a weird look. It was as if she had seen much stranger things in her days. Jared and I probably looked normal in comparison to the customers she had dealt with in the past.

"What time does the first bus to Phoenix leave?" Jared breathlessly asked the woman after having just ran half a mile.

Although Arizona was a neighboring state, it didn't feel like that. We were only about four hours away, but it felt like a lot more because of how difficult our circumstances made traveling. I wished Jared's aunt had decided to live in Los Angeles, instead. It sure would have made this journey a lot easier.

The woman working the ticket counter pointed her finger in the direction behind us, showing Jared and me the current bus schedule. "There's a bus headed to Phoenix at noon tomorrow," she explained.

"Noon?" Jared repeated. "Is there anything that can get us at least close to Phoenix that leaves in the next five minutes?"

The lady behind the window groaned, rolled her eyes, and pointed to the schedule behind us again.

"Okay, fine," Jared muttered after scanning the schedule. "We'll take two tickets for the bus to Vegas."

"Sorry, I can't get you on that bus," she responded.

"Why not? The bus leaves at 1:30 p.m.," Jared exclaimed. "It's 1:21 p.m."

"We stop selling tickets fifteen minutes before the scheduled departure time," she said.

I looked at Jared's face, and for the first time, I actually saw panic in his eyes. He had maintained a strong demeanor throughout the entire trip, but I could see defeat start to creep into his expression. We were almost out of time, and options. It wouldn't be long before the cops logically concluded that the bus station would be the perfect spot to run to. If we didn't get on that bus to Vegas, we would most likely end up in handcuffs. I looked at the bus schedule again, as that seemed to be the key to us getting out of here.

"Thank you for your time," I said to the woman while dragging Jared away from the ticket counter. He was reluctant to walk away, but when I yanked him a little harder, he eventually complied.

"What are you doing?" Jared whispered as we walked back outside, "We have to get out of here. We have no other choice."

"I know," I replied, searching for bus number seven, "and that's exactly what we are going to do."

I grabbed Jared's hand and strutted as casually as I could to the line formed near the bus I was looking for. We were in the back, but we didn't stick out at all. Our beach attire and crazy wigs actually fit in with everyone else waiting in line, as they were also dressed in similar outfits. I wasn't surprised, though. I wouldn't expect anything less from the other people who were also on their way to Las Vegas.

"Elise, we can't get on this bus. We don't have a ticket," Jared reasoned.

"Like you said," I uttered, "we don't have any other choice."

However long it took to check roughly twenty more passengers' tickets was how much longer I had to come up with our next move. I knew that we needed to get on that bus. I just didn't know how we were going to do that.

"Maybe we could steal someone else's ticket," I brainstormed. "Or maybe the bus driver will understand our situation."

I immediately shut down every idea that popped in my head, as they all ended up with either us committing another crime or revealing our identities as wanted criminals.

"I know what we have to do," Jared whispered from behind me. I could hear him swallow the lump in his throat, and his voice was shaky as if he was worried about how the next few moments were about to unfold. "Do you trust me?"

I turned to him and saw the worry on his face. "Of course, I do," I responded.

"Then promise me, when the driver walks away," Jared continued, "you will sneak onto the bus."

"I promise," I answered, confused. "But why would he leave the bus?"

I observed the driver at the entrance of the bus, checking each passenger's ticket before they walked on. There was no way he was going to leave his position. We were scheduled to leave in about five minutes, and he seemed in a hurry to get everyone on.

"Jared, why would he leave the bus?" I asked again when he didn't answer, but when I turned back around to face him, he was lying on the ground.

"Jared!" I screamed, looking at his limp body on the pavement. "Help! Someone please help!"

Everyone in line turned to face us when they heard my shriek. A few rushed over to help, crouching by his side, and trying to feel for a pulse.

"I don't know what happened," I cried out. "One minute we were talking, and then the next thing I know, he's passed out!"

Tears were streaming down my face, as I watched strangers try everything in their power to help Jared, but he didn't move.

"What's going on here?" a raspy voice next to me questioned.

A man with a short stature was staring at Jared on the ground, who I quickly recognized as the bus driver—the bus driver who was no longer guarding the bus. I realized I had severely misjudged Jared's acting abilities. Although his improv could use a little work, his fainting skills were superb. I followed through with my promise to Jared and carefully tiptoed away from the crowd of people, walking onto the bus undetected. The passengers that were already on board were too busy looking outside the window to notice someone new had gotten on. I immediately went to the back, not wanting to be near the bus driver, and found an open seat.

I figured I'd joined the other curious passengers who were watching the scene unfold, so I peered out the window and watched strangers continue to tend to Jared. He had resumed consciousness, but he was acting groggy. Two large men helped him stand up, and they gingerly walked him in the direction of the bus. Jared had one arm around each of them as they slowly assisted him.

"Thank you, fellas," Jared croaked when he finally made it on. "The heat must've gotten to me."

Jared was eagerly scanning the passengers on board, so I briefly waved my hand in the air so that he could find me.

"You sure you are going to be okay?" one of the men who had helped him on asked.

"Yeah, I'll be alright," Jared replied. "I'm just going to go sit with my wife. She'll keep an eye on me."

Jared slowly headed toward the back and dramatically plopped down next to me when he made it to the seat.

"I had better win an Oscar for that performance," he stated, still pretending to recover from his recent incident.

"I think you definitely deserve an award after that," I proudly agreed. "I like how all your fake scenarios include me being your wife."

"Well, hopefully one day that part of the story won't have to be made up," he revealed.

Jared was lying against my shoulder, so he couldn't see my blushed cheeks or giddy smile.

I didn't think men like him existed, especially one that I had met through a reality television show, but Jared was something special. I kissed the top of his head to let him know that the feeling was mutual. He continued to rest against my shoulder, and I wasn't sure if it was from me playing with his hair or the relief that overcame his body when the bus finally pulled away, but after a few minutes into the drive, Jared was fast asleep. I was exhausted, too, but I wanted to soak in the moment for as long as I could. It was the first time since we had started our escape that I actually felt a sense of peace. I knew we weren't in the clear yet, as we still had to find a way from Las Vegas to Phoenix, but we were one step closer. I was also just happy to still have Jared by my side. For the split second that I thought he had actually passed out, I felt a part of my heart crumble away. It was in that moment when I realized that my life wouldn't be the same without him.

My eyes were starting to get heavy and I began to yawn, but I still wasn't ready to fall asleep. I wasn't ready to leave behind the brief moment of bliss that I was experiencing. I had finally found someone who was literally willing to lay their life on the ground for me. I was fully in love with the man who was currently snoring and drooling on my shoulder. In the same way that he laid down on the pavement for me, I vowed to protect his safety, too. No matter what it took or what it cost, I wanted to do everything in my power to keep him out of harm's way. He not only had my heart, but my loyalty, as well.

***

I woke up to the sound of the bus driver announcing a brief pit stop. As much as I wanted to get to Las Vegas, I was happy for the opportunity to use a proper bathroom and stretch my legs. We turned into a large rest area, and judging by the price of gas, it seemed we hadn't even left the state of California yet. The squeaky brakes and sudden jolt when the bus finally came to a complete stop interrupted Jared's nap. He lazily lifted his head off my shoulder, but a string of drool still connected us together.

"Did you sleep well?" I asked, giggling at him trying to make sense of his surroundings. He felt the corner of his mouth and noticed the pool of drool on me.

"Sorry about that," he apologized, wiping away at the wet spot, "but that was the best nap of my life. Have you ever thought about becoming a pillow?"

"Almost every single day," I sarcastically replied.

The other passengers began to exit the bus, appearing very eager at the chance for some fresh air.

"Where are we?" Jared questioned as he stared out the window.

"Not Vegas," I responded. "Want to stretch your legs for a bit?"

"I think my legs have done enough today," he uttered, pulling out the dwindling wad of the cash from his pocket. "Want to split a candy bar, though?"

We didn't have much money left, but if we didn't eat, then Jared might actually pass out.

"I'd love to," I affirmed, standing up from my seat.

Jared walked out first, and I quickly followed closely behind him. A few passengers stayed on the bus, but most of them headed for the restrooms or opted to just walk around aimlessly.

"Here," Jared said, handing me a five dollar bill. "Grab whatever you want. I am going to use that payphone over there and call my Aunt Laura. She still has no idea that we are in trouble and need her help."

"Good idea. Don't forget to remind her that you won't be showing up alone," I said.

Jared pulled me closer to him and kissed me five or six times before finally pulling away.

"How could I forget to mention my wife?" he stated with a wink.

I watched him walk toward the payphone near the side of the building before walking into the gas station. It was pretty crowded since a bunch of people had just unloaded from a large bus, but most of them were in line for the bathroom. Therefore, I had the freedom to walk up and down the aisle without any interruptions. Fortunately, Jared had given me enough to buy a small bag of chips and a candy bar, so I was pretty pleased to be able to purchase two items. It was far from a gourmet meal, but I knew Jared would appreciate the extra calories.

The line for the women's bathrooms was pretty long, but it moved fairly quick so it didn't take long for me to complete my mission in the gas station. I was surprised to have been able to make a purchase and complete a trip to the bathroom without much time passing by. I was probably in and out of the gas station within ten minutes. Jared was still on the phone when I walked outside, so I decided to head in his direction. As I got closer, I noticed he looked pretty upset. It may have even seemed like he was in an argument with his aunt by the way his voice was raised. I wasn't close enough to hear exactly what he was saying, but he definitely wasn't talking in a friendly tone.

Jared didn't notice me at first, but when he finally saw me, he quickly whispered something into the phone and hung up.

"Is everything okay?" I asked, observing his distraught behavior.

He started pacing back and forth frantically, muttering things I couldn't hear under his breath.

"My aunt is furious," Jared finally admitted. "She thinks I'm making the biggest mistake of my life."

"How?" I questioned. "We had no other choice. Brent was going to ruin the whole show!"

"She said that because it's his production, he can do whatever he wants," Jared explained.

"Is she still willing to help us?" I nervously asked.

Jared's expression turned even more distraught.

"She said she's only willing to help me ..." he shakily answered. "She thinks that this is your fault, and that I'm throwing my life away for a girl I barely even know."

My heart dropped at the idea of having to face this situation on my own. I just always pictured going through this journey with Jared that I never imagined what it would be like without having his support.

"Don't worry, I'm not going to leave you behind," Jared shared.

"Jared ..." I began, "if she's not willing to help me, you still need to meet with her. At least one of us needs to get out of this mess."

Jared grabbed my hands into his and gently kissed the top of each of them.

"Life isn't worth living if it isn't with you," he started, "and problems aren't worth facing if I don't have you by my side. I'll worry about my aunt later, but for now, we are still going to go to Arizona ... together."

I smiled as Jared gave me a quick peck. Nothing seemed as scary when I was with him. Even running away from the police wasn't as nerve-racking when I had my favorite person by my side.

"Elise," Jared whispered, interlocking his fingers with mine. "We need to leave."

"Okay," I answered, walking back toward the bus.

"No," Jared demanded as he pulled me in the opposite direction. "This way."

He led me in the direction of the woods behind the gas station. Our brisk walk suddenly turned into a light jog, and I was curious as to why he was taking us away from our only way of getting out of here. Before we were fully out of sight, I turned around and saw the red and blue flashing lights of a police car surrounding the bus. Someone must have recognized us and notified the authorities, which meant a picture of us was probably circulating the internet and all the local television channels.

We had been on the run for a few days now, but it felt like we weren't any closer to Phoenix. I was starting to wonder if we would truly ever find a way out of the hole that we had dug ourselves in. Maybe Jared's aunt was right. This whole situation might all be my fault, and I simply dragged Jared down with me. If you truly love someone, you let them go, right? Perhaps it was time to finally just let Jared go.

6

Episode 6: Slumber Party

JARED

I didn't know how the police knew where to find us, how long they would stay at the gas station, or if they were searching the woods where we were hiding. However, my first priority was making sure Elise was safe. I led her deep into the trees until I was certain that nobody was following us. We started our hike with plenty of daylight, but we had been trudging on for hours so when we stumbled upon a clearing, I decided that we would finally put a cease to our long journey. It's not like we had much of a choice. We couldn't just keep walking. Neither of us knew how vast the forest was. It was also important that we didn't stray too far away from the gas station, as we would most likely have to return there tomorrow. Honestly, it felt like any option was a dead end, but my motivation to bring Elise to safety was at the forefront of my mind, and, therefore, guided most of my decisions.

It was still in our best interest to find a way to Phoenix, even though my Aunt Laura was adamant about only helping me. I didn't expect Elise's trip to the gas station to only last a few minutes, so I was surprised when I turned around and saw her staring at me arguing on the phone. She looked concerned, and I almost didn't even want to reveal my aunt's true sentiments, but I could never lie to her. It truly didn't matter how she felt about Elise anyway, as I was going to make sure that she got the assistance that she needed. Elise wasn't just my other half, she was my whole heart, and there was no way I was just going to leave her on her own. I'd figure out all the logistics at a later point in time, as we still needed to find a way to get to Arizona, but for now, we just needed to learn how to become one with nature.

"This should be a good spot," I announced, observing the small clearing in the woods.

"We're going to sleep out here?" Elise questioned in a panic.

I would have rather spent the night in an expensive hotel, ordering room service until our stomachs hurt, but unfortunately, we did not have that luxury.

"It's only temporary," I explained, comforting Elise. "We'll stay out here tonight, and then in the morning, we will head back to the gas station and figure out our next steps. But we can't risk going back tonight. The police are probably still waiting for us."

Elise ripped the mangled green wig off her head and itched her scalp. I took mine off, too, as there was no point in hiding our identities in the middle of nowhere. My once shimmering, purple bob was currently a tangled mess of hair and leaves. Hopefully, Victoria wouldn't be too mad when we returned her disheveled wigs. At least we had kept her pink car in good condition.

"So, what do we do now?" Elise inquired. "I've never been camping before."

"Neither have I," I admitted, "but I have seen a lot of movies about it, and usually they start by building a fire. Let's search the woods for some sticks and anything else that we might need. Maybe we'll find a warm blanket and fluffy pillows somewhere."

I tried to make light of the situation with a little joke, but Elise didn't laugh. We were running on very little sleep and barely any food, and tonight wasn't going to help that. I'd love to take Elise on a proper vacation once all this was over. I was sad that our first nights sleeping together outside of *Heartbreak Beach* were in a motel and a dark, cold forest, but one day I'd make it up to her.

"I'll search over here, and you can head over to that area," I instructed, pointing to a part of the forest that seemed the least frightening. "Let me know if you find anything."

She took direction well and immediately started walking off in order to find some firewood.

"Elise," I called out, before she went away. "Don't go too far."

She nodded her head in agreement, before heading toward her designated search area.

We could go a few more days running on only gas station candy bars and chips. Elise and I could probably even last quite a bit longer without much sleep. However, as soon as we lost our spirit was when I would know that we were in serious trouble. The twinkles in Elise's eyes were starting to fade, along with the hope she had about making it out of here. I wanted to restore all her faith that the hard part was done, and that this whole mess was almost over, but I was also starting to doubt myself. We were running low on money, and I didn't know how well we would sleep tonight, but hopelessness would get to us far before the exhaustion would. We needed to keep our spirits high. Brent Knox may not have gotten to us physically, but he was definitely getting to us mentally.

I hoped that Elise's side of the woods was more plentiful than mine because I barely managed to find anything salvageable. The few sticks I found barely even counted as firewood and would probably crumble under the force of my hands before they were even used to maintain a fire. Surviving in the wilderness looked a lot easier on television than it actually was in real life, but from my time filming *Heartbreak Beach*, I quickly realized that depictions on TV were far from the truth.

"Jared!" I heard my name shouted in the distance. "I found something!"

I immediately ran in the direction of Elise's voice, dropping my sticks in the process. I figured it was better to show up empty-handed than present the pathetic pieces of wood that I had gathered.

When I made it to Elise, I found her standing over a worn-out duffel bag. It was covered in dirt and leaves, and appeared as though it had been in that exact spot for months. At this point, it was basically a part of the forest.

"What do you think is in it?" she whispered, staring at the bag.

"Only one way to find out," I answered, lunging for it.

"Jared, stop!" Elise shouted while holding me back. "What if it's something dangerous?"

I couldn't imagine what could be hiding in a dirty sports bag in the middle of the forest, but I appreciated her concern for me.

"What if it's filled with poisonous spiders or a venomous snake?" she asked.

I doubted those creatures preferred to house themselves in a confined bag, but her outlandish worries were actually starting to scare me. A dangerous animal hiding inside never crossed my mind, but now I was starting to become skeptical.

"Let's hit it with a stick first," Elise voiced. "We can see if it will move."

I still wasn't convinced that there was a deadly animal hiding inside, but I also didn't want to take any chances.

Elise's side of the forest was definitely more resourceful than mine, as it didn't take me that long to find a broken branch that was long enough for me to poke the bag with while maintaining a safe distance from it. In the rare case that a venomous snake or poisonous spider did crawl out, I'd have plenty of time to put Elise on my back and run for our lives.

I kept telling myself that I was being silly and that the bag was most likely filled with leaves, but I was very hesitant to nudge it. Elise was hiding behind me, peeking over my shoulder to see what would happen next. Eventually, I just decided to swallow my fear, as I couldn't look afraid in front of the girl that I was planning on marrying one day. I wanted her to always view me as her protector.

The bag stood still as I hovered my stick around it. I figured if there was actually an animal in there, it would have already moved by now. We were continuing to lose light and didn't have much time left to build a fire, so it was now or never. I closed one eye out of fear, but kept one open as I was as curious as Elise as to what was going to happen next. I slowly aimed the stick at the duffel bag and gently tapped it. I jumped back in anticipation of the worst and almost tripped over Elise who was behind me, but nothing happened. The bag didn't even move an inch. The stillness gave me more confidence, so I took the stick and poked it even harder. Again, there was no movement. Just to be totally certain, I started whacking it with all my force. Now, if there actually was a creature in there, it would've probably been dead by now.

"I think we're good," I whispered to Elise, who had just witnessed my attack on the dirty duffel.

"Should we open it now?" she asked.

"I'll do it," I offered. "Stay right here."

I was ninety-nine percent confident that the contents of the bag were not harmful, but that one percent could be the difference between safety and putting Elise in harm's way, so I made sure she stayed behind. I inched myself closer and closer, until the bag was right at my feet. I gave it one more kick, just to make sure the potential beast inside was truly incapacitated. When the bag still didn't move, I bravely crouched down beside it and reached for the zipper.

"Be careful, Jared," Elise warned in the distance.

I should've kissed her one more time, in case these were my last moments. Instead, I slowly unzipped the bag, revealing the shocking contents inside.

"Elise, come here!" I called out to her.

Elise abruptly jogged over and knelt beside me. She stared at the items inside the bag and began to shuffle through them.

"Matches, granola bars, water, a knife," Elise said, naming out each item, "and a sleeping bag!"

Joy filled her face and the hope that had recently been fading was suddenly restored.

"Hopefully you don't mind getting cozy tonight," I shared, noting that there was only one sleeping bag.

Elise grabbed my face and started kissing me out of excitement. "I'd sleep anywhere with you."

The rest of the bag was filled with leaves and broken sticks. Nothing else was of use.

"We hit the jackpot!" Elise screamed out. "How did we get so lucky?"

I packed up the contents of the bag in order to carry it back to our campsite. Elise was skipping for joy and I couldn't blame her for her happiness. I, too, was excited for the treasures we stumbled upon, however, I wouldn't necessarily consider ourselves lucky. Elise may have deducted that the supplies came from previous campers that had passed through. It was the only spot in the woods that had the perfect flat landscape for a tent, and the clearing provided enough space for a campfire. Unfortunately, the blood that I secretly had to wipe off the knife before putting it into my pocket made me think otherwise. Our campsite may have also doubled as a graveyard, or worse ... a crime scene.

I kept my guard up and the knife on my hip while we walked back to the clearing in the woods. Elise immediately grabbed the jug of water and a granola bar when I put the duffel down, but my main focus was getting a fire started. Elise offered to help me collect some firewood, but after the eerie sight of seeing the bloodied knife, I didn't let her back into the thick of the woods. I just decided I'd settle for what I could find around our campsite, while keeping an eye on Elise. Thankfully, the knife made it easier to gather what I needed as I was able to cut some branches off the surrounding trees. They made for a better base than the flimsy sticks that I had originally gathered. I was also extremely grateful for the matches, as they were critical to helping start a fire. I probably would have just rubbed two sticks together until I got a spark.

After all the work we had done to find a campsite and gather the proper materials, I was finally satisfied once I had a fire going and the sleeping bag was laid out. I decided to hang out by the flames and treat myself to a granola bar and some water. I wanted to relax and admire the hard work I had just completed, but I couldn't settle my nerves down enough. I kept thinking that at any second, something dangerous was going to pop out from behind the trees. The full moon, numerous stars, and the fire were our only sources of light. They were able to illuminate our immediate surroundings, but darkness was still lurking around us. We were surrounded by a pitch black blanket. Even if there was something or someone hiding in the shadows, we surely would not have been able to see it.

Elise let out a giant yawn and began rubbing the crust in her eyes. It was a physically and emotionally exhausting day, and I was also ready to lay my head down.

"Bed time?" I asked, noticing her sleepy eyes.

She didn't verbally answer, but she nodded her head in agreement.

I got up from my spot by the fire and walked over to the sleeping bag. I unzipped it and let Elise climb inside first. When she was comfortable, I carefully slipped in next to her. It was truly a tight squeeze, but it was also comforting being so close to her. I wrapped my arm around her and nestled against her soft skin. I kissed her exposed shoulder, as we were still in our beach attire. Unfortunately, the bag didn't contain extra clothes. Her white beach cover up matched my t-shirt, which now more closely resembled a shade of light brown. It was another rough day on the run, but we got to end it together.

"Goodnight, Elise," I softly spoke against her ear. I tapped my pocket one more time to ensure the knife was still on hand.

"Goodnight, Jared," Elise whispered back.

I wanted to spend the rest of the night talking with her about our future and envisioning our life together after we were finally free from the wrath of Brent Knox, but it didn't take long for exhaustion to consume her body. She fell fast asleep before I could even utter my next words.

"I love you, Elise," I confessed, even though she didn't hear me.

I continued to fight the battle of sleep. As tired as I was, I couldn't let anything happen to her. These woods were capable of a lot more than Elise or I could have prepared for. It was home to ravaging animals and egregious hunters. I was going to let Elise sleep while I stayed awake to make sure she was safe. We were already in a giant mess, and I was going to make it my life's mission to protect her at all costs.

7

Episode 7: Road Trip

ELISE

In any other circumstances, sharing a sleeping bag in the middle of the woods, being cold and hungry, and trying to escape a ruthless producer was a recipe for a horrible night. However, in my case, I slept the best I had in a while. It probably had to do with the fact that I was exhausted from the long hike it took to even get to the campsite, but I believed Jared had a large part in it, too. It was tiring always having to watch my back, but whenever I was in his care, I felt safe. His presence seemed to alleviate all of my worries, which was why I freaked out when I woke up the next morning and he wasn't next to me.

I checked my surroundings, but there was no sign of him. I called out his name, but I heard nothing in return. The worst-case scenarios began to fill my thoughts, however, there didn't appear to be any signs of a struggle, as our campsite was still intact. The duffel bag was still lying in the same spot it had when I fell asleep and nothing appeared to be missing from it. I shouted for Jared a few more times—my voice echoing throughout the forest. Instead of hearing him in return, I heard twigs snapping in the distance. In a quick reaction, I grabbed the water jug for protection. It wasn't going to do much, but with the right hit, it might be able to knock out a small animal ... or human. A few more branches broke off in the distance, and the sound of wood snapping under the force of footsteps was getting closer. I debated zipping myself back up in the sleeping bag, but that was too obvious of a hiding spot. I also thought about running, but I wasn't certain which direction the sound was coming from. I was a sitting duck in the middle of a small clearing in the woods, with only a canteen as a weapon.

My heart thumped, and I tried to quiet it down so that I could hear the sounds coming from deep within the woods—I clearly wasn't alone. I shouted for Jared a few more times, but when I still didn't hear a response,

I prepared myself for the worst. I was by myself, alone, and having to fend for myself against whatever was about to emerge.

"I have a water bottle and I'm not afraid to use it!" I screamed, hoping it would deter the danger that was coming for me.

I was still unsure of which direction the footsteps were coming from, until a loud snap echoed from behind me. I quickly whipped my head around, ready to fight off my attacker.

"Woah, there," Jared said as he approached our campsite. "I come in peace."

"Jared!" I shouted, running over to him. I wanted to hug him, but his arms were full of broken branches.

"Sorry, I didn't mean to scare you," he apologized. "I tried to collect some firewood before you woke up. These California mornings can get pretty cold."

He walked over to the dying fire and laid the additional wood he had found on top of it. The duffel was nearby, so he grabbed the matches out of it and reignited the fire. The wood cracked as it began to burn, and a rush of heat radiated from it. I took a seat next to him and cuddled up against his warm body.

"Why didn't you answer when I shouted your name?" I asked, soaking up the heat.

"Honestly, I got lost and the sound of your voice was leading me back to the campsite," he responded. "I didn't want to shout back and disturb whatever beasts were still sleeping in the forest."

"Are there bears in these woods?" I cautiously questioned, nervous about how much danger we were actually in. I could tell we weren't as safe as Jared had led me to believe, but I knew he just didn't want me to be afraid.

"Let's not worry about that right now," he replied, handing me a granola bar. "After we warm up, we can head back to the gas station."

"Do you think the gas station has showers?" I inquired, sniffing my dirty clothes. "Or maybe a laundry machine?"

I took a bite of my granola bar and sip of the water. I knew the journey back would be tiring and I wanted to gain as much strength as I could before the long hike.

"The gas station probably does not have that, but my aunt will," Jared answered. "We should be there by the afternoon."

Jared seemed confident about the possibility of getting to Arizona today, so I refrained from questioning his plan. He seemed to have everything under control.

We drank the rest of the water and split the last granola bar before making the walk back to the gas station.

***

Oddly enough, the return trip didn't seem as bad as I thought it would be. I figured I was under such duress when we first headed to the campsite, that it made the hike feel longer. However, this morning, we reached the gas station before my feet even became sore.

I was relieved to have made it to our destination, but apparently our journey wasn't over. Jared held on to my hand, and instead of leading me toward the gas pumps, we walked toward the road.

"Where are we going?" I asked. Although I fully trusted Jared and his plan to get us out of here, I was confused when we passed up the gas station and began walking alongside the road.

"We're hitchhiking," Jared responded casually, as if that was a normal activity.

"Hitchhiking?" I shouted, appalled that this was what his plan consisted of.

He stuck out his arm and tried to flag down each car that passed by.

"Jared, we can't hitchhike," I relayed. "We're going to get kidnapped."

"Don't worry, I won't let anything bad happen to you," he stated.

"But, Jared," I interjected.

"Just stick out your hand," he directed.

I was reluctant to try and get a stranger to drive us to our destination, but I didn't have any better ideas so I just did what I was told. Each vehicle that drove by was a potential solution to reaching Arizona, so I attempted to wave them down. However, it seemed as if nobody was going to stop. I didn't blame them, as I probably wouldn't have picked up two hitchhikers, either.

"This isn't working," I exclaimed, feeling defeated after not even a single car slowed down.

"You're right," Jared agreed.

I wasn't expecting him to admit that his plan had failed, but he put his arm down and stopped flagging down cars. I was disappointed that we would have to come up with a different game plan, but was relieved that we wouldn't have to get a ride from a potential serial killer. I wanted to be a contributing member to our escape, so I tried to think of something else we could do, but my thoughts came to an abrupt stop when Jared jumped in front of a vehicle, forcing it to slam on its breaks.

"Jared!" I shouted, "You almost got killed!"

"Well, you said it wasn't working," he explained, "so I had to try something else."

In his defense, he indeed got a car to stop. However, I would have rather him attempted something that didn't involve risking his life.

"Hey, man, are you crazy?" the driver yelled after rolling down his window.

"Just a little," Jared affirmed, walking over to the car. "Think we could get a ride?"

The driver was a burly middle-aged man with a dark beard. He seemed furious that we had interrupted his drive, and I did not think this was the appropriate time to ask him if we could join him on his journey.

"Well, unless you're headed to Dallas, then I can't help you out," the angry driver remarked.

"Perfect," Jared voiced.

Jared reached through the passenger window that was rolled down, unlocked the door, and began to hop in the car.

"What are you doing?" the strange man shouted. "Get out of my car!"

"We're headed to Phoenix," Jared informed the man as he reached in the back seat and opened the door for me to get in. "It's on the way to Dallas."

I tiptoed over to the car, hesitant to get inside.

"It's okay," Jared said, encouraging me to get in.

I really did not want to hop in the vehicle, but the last thing I wanted was to be separated from Jared, and he was already inside. Therefore, I reluctantly took the seat behind him and shut the car door.

"What is going on?" the driver questioned. "I cannot just take you both to Phoenix."

"Sure you can," Jared replied confidently. He reached inside his pocket and gave the man the rest of the cash we had left. "For gas."

The strange man groaned but took the money from Jared and began to drive off.

"Next time you jump in front of my car," he began, "I'm running you over."

"Deal," Jared noted, peering at me through the rearview mirror.

I tried to smile through the anxiety, but driving across state lines with someone we didn't know was definitely a cause for panic. Jared seemed calm and collected, but he liked to act brave around me. I was sure he was freaking out on the inside, too.

"I'm George and that's Rose," Jared introduced, continuing to utilize our fake names. I was surprised he had remembered them this time.

"Hugo," the driver grunted.

"Hugo?" Jared repeated with a slight chuckle. "I've never heard that one before."

"You got a problem with my name?" he fired back.

"No, no problem at all," Jared replied. "You just don't look like a Hugo. I would've guessed your name was something along the lines of ... Wallace."

"Wallace?" Hugo repeated.

"Yeah, Wallace was my grandma's dog's name before he got hit by car. He had an overgrown beard and crusty eyes just like yours," Jared explained.

I didn't think it was possible for Jared to anger the driver any further, but he had successfully managed to do that. Hugo's scowl seemed to intensify after each time Jared spoke. It was probably in Jared's best interest to keep quiet.

"Thank you so much for rescuing us, Hugo," I piped up from the back-seat. "We're actually headed to Phoenix for a family reunion. We arrived at the gas station by bus, but I guess we took a little too long in the bathroom and it left us. Our wallets and phones are still on it."

Hugo didn't respond. I didn't think he necessarily cared for our cover story, but at least his expression had softened a tiny bit.

"Hey, Hugo. Do you think we could use your cell phone real quick?" Jared asked.

The angry scowl had returned to his face at the sound of Jared's voice. It was evident that Hugo didn't like Jared very much, but he still handed over his phone.

While Jared was making a phone call to his aunt, I decided to make small talk with the driver. The last thing I wanted was to continue to upset the person who was taking us to safety.

"So, Hugo," I began, as Jared was updating his aunt on our where-abouts. "Why are you headed to Dallas?"

He didn't respond at first. Instead, he just looked at me through the mirror as if contemplating whether I was trustworthy enough to talk to. Ultimately, he must've decided that I wasn't a threat since he eventually answered.

"A woman," he mumbled.

"Oh, a woman. Is she your girlfriend? Your wife?" I inquired.

Hugo was hesitant to answer again. This time, instead of responding, he opened the middle console. I was hoping that Jared still had the knife on him, as I wasn't certain what Hugo was about to retrieve. However, I breathed a sigh of relief when he handed me a small box. I shakily took it from him. When I opened it, a shining engagement ring was nestled inside.

"Oh my goodness!" I shrieked. "She's going to love it!"

"Love what?" Jared asked, as I handed the ring box back to Hugo. He had just ended the call with his aunt and was joining the middle of our conversation.

I knew I had somewhat earned Hugo's trust, and I didn't want to break it, so I refrained from divulging the details of what we had talked about. If Hugo really wanted to share his engagement plans with Jared, he would've done so on his own.

"So, what did your aunt say?" I asked, changing the subject.

"She told us to meet her at her office," Jared explained. "I told her we would be there this afternoon."

"What's the name of her workplace again?" I questioned, pulling out the map that Jared had given me. It was hard to read, but the law firm was clearly circled in red.

"Bernstein & Becker Law Firm," Jared relayed.

Hugo kept his eyes on the road. He didn't seem interested in partaking in any conversation that Jared was involved in. I got him to open up a little, but he immediately shut down once Jared spoke up. I felt bad that we had bombarded his trip to propose to his girlfriend by making him stop in Phoenix first. Hopefully, there was a way that we could make it up to him other than giving him a couple bucks for gas.

Thankfully, Hugo wasn't angered any further as Jared kept his mouth shut for the majority of the trip. I stared out the window and slowly watched California's tropical terrain turn into a desolate desert. I may have even fallen asleep at some point because we seemed to approach our destination faster than I had expected. As soon as I saw the sign notifying us that we were crossing state lines into Arizona, a rush of excitement ran through me.

"Should only be a couple hours from this point," Jared noted when he saw the sign, as well.

The long journey was finally coming to an end. We had slept in a bug-infested motel, camped in the middle of nowhere, and hitchhiked across state lines in order to get to this point. An overwhelming sense of relief came across me as it seemed nothing could stop us now.

"Hugo, could you stop at the next gas station?" Jared asked. "I need to use the restroom."

"I'll stop when we get a little closer," Hugo stated.

All Hugo wanted to do was reach his girlfriend, and we were delaying his arrival.

"I need to use the bathroom, now," Jared warned. "I can't hold it any longer. Unless you want your passenger seat to be soaked, then I'd pull over."

Hugo muttered something under his breath, but ultimately ended up turning into the rest stop that Jared had pointed out. He must have really had to go because as soon as the car was parked, Jared flung his door open.

"I'll be right back," Jared notified, as he raced toward the bathroom.

It was just Hugo and I, alone in his old station wagon. Usually, I would have been super uncomfortable, but I wasn't as afraid of him knowing that a woman was the motivation behind him driving across the country. A man who would do anything for love was not someone that I feared.

Since we were already there, Hugo decided to fill up for gas while we waited for Jared. We pulled out of the parking spot that was right in front of the door and found an empty pump on the far side of the rest stop. When Hugo exited the vehicle, I got out as well as I didn't want to be the only one in the car. However, I quickly ducked my head back inside when I saw a police car pull into the rest stop. It parked in the same spot that we were originally in, which meant that they were now right in front of the bathrooms. I didn't have a way to warn him, but even if I did, there wouldn't have been enough time because as soon as the officers got out of the car, Jared walked back outside.

8

Episode 8: Unbreakable Bond

JARED

I was grateful that I was finally able to relieve myself after Hugo's apprehension about pulling over to the nearest rest stop. I didn't know if he just wanted me to suffer or didn't believe me, but I was fully prepared to douse the passenger seat of his car with my bodily fluids. The water from the canteen had finally made its way through my system, and although it was an untimely bathroom break, the relief of finally seeing the sign that indicated our arrival in Arizona must have excited me a little too much. My bladder had a mind of its own, and when it had to go, it had to go.

The cleanliness of the restroom actually surprised me, as I didn't expect a random toilet right across the state border to smell like roses. However, I wouldn't have been surprised if it had actually smelled like my brother Marshall's smelly gym socks. I was in such a good mood that my senses were starting to trick me. I heard birds chirping, smelled flowers, and felt a cool breeze even in the middle of a desert. My eyes were even starting to imagine things. I swore I saw a wedding ring on the floor of the bathroom. At one point, I even believed that I was at the altar, waiting for my beautiful soon-to-be wife to walk down the aisle. The love between Elise and I was indeed magical, but not even Houdini himself could have conjured up the wizardry to trick my mind into thinking that Hugo's old station wagon had turned into a police car. As soon as I walked outside and saw two law enforcement officers standing in front of the squad car that was parked where Hugo once was, I immediately turned around and ran back inside.

Unfortunately, the rest stop's bathroom wasn't suited for an escape. There wasn't a giant opening that I could easily squeeze through or a secret back door, however, there was a tiny window that I could see the cops through, as well as, the gas pump that Hugo was filling up at. Elise was in the car, but I could see her head poking through the window, checking to see if I had been recognized or not. She seemed distraught, but not enough for me to assume that my identity had been compromised. The female officer was leaning against the car, but the male cop who was once next to her, was nowhere to be found. I didn't have to guess where he was headed though, as I heard footsteps leading up to the bathroom. The cop's shoes thudded against the concrete leading up to the door, and the keys on his hip jangled with each move he made. Thankfully, I managed to scurry into a stall before he entered. I couldn't imagine what Elise was probably thinking right now. She was most likely debating whether she should run into the men's restroom or not, but I knew she was smart enough to wait it out.

I could see the officer at the urinal through the crack in the stall, and it was clear that arresting two runaways was not on his agenda today. He was just on his regular patrol, stopping for a bathroom break. When he zipped his pants back up, he walked over to the bathroom sink and adjusted his hair in the mirror. Without even attempting to wash his hands, he walked back outside, not even aware that a fugitive was hiding in the bathroom behind him.

I waited a few more seconds before creeping out of the stall and racing back toward the small window. I needed to wait for the police to leave before I headed back to Hugo's car, but they were still standing outside, having a conversation amongst themselves. In my opinion, there wasn't much to talk about at a rest stop in Arizona, but apparently there was a lot on their minds. At first, I was getting annoyed at their small talk, but I began to freak out once I saw them end their discussion and walk toward Hugo's car. I felt like I was a quick thinker, but in that moment, I didn't have a plan. I couldn't just let the cops reach the station wagon as there was no place for Elise to hide. She surely would have been caught. Love was all about sacrifice, and what kind of man would I be if I let my woman go down without a fight? Therefore, against maybe other people's better judgment, I ran out of the bathroom in an obnoxious attempt to deter the officers from taking one more step toward Elise.

"Looking for me?" I yelled out, calling their attention away from Hugo's car.

The officers stopped their pursuit and turned around to see me walking out of the restroom. The female officer whispered something into her radio. I couldn't exactly make out what she was saying, but shortly after she spoke, the male cop raced toward me. It wasn't an ideal situation to have the police chase after me in ninety degree weather while I was in sandals, but I ran like Elise's life depended on it. I couldn't have been certain of what would have happened if the officers had made it to Hugo's vehicle. Perhaps, they were simply asking for directions or inquiring about the price of gas, but I couldn't risk it. I'd never be able to forgive myself if something happened to her.

The sandy terrain made it difficult to create distance. My shoes were sliding across the grains, and it felt like I had to take ten steps before I could move a considerable amount. I could hear the clanking of handcuffs getting closer as the officer was clearly having a better time running in the sand than I was. I was fully prepared to be tackled and have my face in the ground in a matter of seconds. My legs were moving as fast as they could, but any hope of getting away was completely lost—this was the end of my journey.

"Officer Cordell, this is Officer Nelly," I heard the radio cackle. "The main target has been identified in the vehicle at the gas pump."

Upon hearing the update, Officer Cordell immediately gave up on chasing me and returned his focus back toward the gas pump. He left me in the dust to assist his partner in subduing the real target, Elise Rosenberg. The tables had turned, and I was now the one chasing the officer. My sandals were still preventing me from getting to my destination in the amount of time that I desired, but my motivation to save Elise was propelling me forward.

Unfortunately, Officer Cordell reached Officer Nelly way before I had. Their hands were on their weapons, as they crept toward the vehicle, screaming at Elise and Hugo. Their hands were raised, and they held them outside the car to show the cops that they were not a threat. The police continued to tiptoe their way toward them, and I was running out of time.

I knew Elise had been the main target this whole time. Even though I was the one who stole Victoria's car, I knew Brent was going to find a way to ensure that the majority of our crimes were pinned on her. He had a personal vendetta against her for ruining the *Heartbreak Beach* finale that he had so carefully thought out in his head. This wasn't about the stolen car or running away from set. This whole mess was because a producer's ego was hurt, and he wanted to take revenge on the person who had gone against his orders. In all of his years of working on television shows, I bet nobody ever had the guts to stand up to him like Elise had. The cast, the crew, and even I were under his strict control, but there was one fiery redhead who couldn't be tamed. She was Brent's kryptonite, and I had to save her.

There wasn't much to work with in the middle of the Arizona desert. Unless a rattlesnake decided to scare the cops away or I became crazy enough to utilize the knife in my pocket, there weren't very many options left. However, I needed to rescue Elise. After some quick thinking, I frantically took my shirt off, wrapped my fist in the cloth, and shouted random sounds as I ran toward the squad car. I caught the attention of Officer Nelly and Officer Cordell, and probably anyone else within a five-mile radius as my screams were loud enough to be heard all the way back to California. I jumped onto the hood of the cop car, and began punching the windshield with the hand that was wrapped in my shirt. I really had watched too much television, as the thin piece of fabric did not protect me from the pain that was shooting through my arm as glass was flying everywhere and blood was trickling onto the damaged windshield.

"Go, Elise!" I screamed, while continuing to bash the glass. "Get to my aunt and save yourself!"

I was quickly yanked off the squad car and thrown onto the hot pavement. My knuckles were bloody and stinging with sharp pains, and my back took a severe blow when it smacked against the ground. However, the sound of tires screeching away made it all worth it.

"Jared, no!" Elise screamed through the open window of the station wagon that sped past.

Elise had probably thought I was being annoying on the drive over here. She was most likely unhappy with how I had treated Hugo, the man who had graciously given us a ride to Arizona, but it was all for a reason. I knew there would come a moment where Hugo would have to choose between me or Elise, and I wanted to ensure that when that time came, it would be an easy decision for him. I needed him to choose Elise. I'd handle whatever punishment was handed to me. If spending the rest of my life in jail was my future, then so be it, as long as it protected Elise.

Officer Cordell flipped me onto my stomach and drove his knee into my back while Officer Nelly put the cuffs on me. They dragged me off the ground and flung me into the back of the car as they called for backup. Evidently, they couldn't drive away with a busted windshield, so I was left to sit in the backseat while another vehicle was on its way.

"You just ruined your life, kid," Officer Cordell stated from outside the vehicle. He was kind enough to roll the windows down so I wouldn't melt in the hot car, but he was probably more concerned about making sure that

I knew my life would never be the same and that I would pay for damaging his precious car.

There was nothing I could say to get myself out of this one, so I just quietly sat there, hoping that Elise would reach my Aunt Laura sooner rather than later. I hoped her law degree had allowed her to dabble in topics outside of just entertainment because I was in real trouble now.

"Running away. Damaging police property," Officer Cordell continued on. "And for what? A girl?"

I knew he was just trying to get a reaction out of me, so I refrained from engaging in the conversation.

"Let me guess," he said. "You ran away with her. She told you that she loves you and doesn't want to be with anyone else. I bet she's even got you thinking about forever with her."

I kept my eyes trained on the back of the seat in front of me, avoiding any eye contact with him.

"I'll give you a little insight into your future," Officer Cordell explained. "You're going to jail for the rest of your life, and your little girlfriend is going to go find a new guy to run off into the sunset with."

I scowled, still refusing to respond, but his comments were striking a nerve. I knew he could tell that Elise was my soft spot.

"He's a quiet one." Officer Cordell chuckled to his partner. "Must be why she likes him."

I most likely would've exploded if he had poked any more fun at Elise's and my relationship, but Officer Nelly had a larger agenda in mind. She walked closer to the car and crouched lower to talk to me.

"Where's the girl headed?" she asked. "What was your plan?"

I wasn't happy to hear that there was still an immediate urge to arrest Elise, but I was glad to know that they hadn't found her yet. Instead of answering, I just shrugged my shoulders.

"Sir, if you do not answer you will be charged for aiding and abetting a fugitive. Now, where is she going?" Officer Nelly asked again.

I returned her question with another shrug of the shoulders. Officer Cordell jumped in and started screaming at me in a classic good cop, bad cop routine.

"Kid, if you want to see the sun again, you better answer the question!" he threatened.

Still, I remained silent.

"You are looking at serious charges and we can get you a deal," Officer Nelly said, hopping back in the conversation and utilizing her good cop role. "All you have to do is tell me where the girl is headed."

Elise was a wanted woman—not just by me, but by the cops, as well. When her stunning beauty took my breath away, I knew I would have to defend her from all the men out there. I just never thought I would also have to defend her from the cops. Although the sound of making all these charges disappear sounded great, I had already made a promise to myself to protect Elise.

"She's headed," I began. "She's headed to ..."

The cops stared at me like drooling dogs about to feast on a juicy steak. They were so eager to hear my answer, that they didn't even notice that their backup squad car had arrived to transport me. The officers just looked at me, ignoring their surroundings and awaiting my response.

"Well, spit it out," Officer Cordell urged.

Officer Nelly gave him a slight nudge in his side, seemingly in order to prevent him from pressuring me any further and risking me not saying anything at all.

"Where is she headed?" Officer Nelly repeated kindly.

"She's headed to *Heartbreak Beach*," I finally answered.

"*Heartbreak Beach*?" Officer Cordell questioned. "Where is that?"

"The place where I realized that life truly isn't worth living unless you have the love of your life with you by your side," I shared.

Officer Cordell groaned. He opened the car door, yanked me out of the damaged car, and threw me into the vehicle that had just arrived.

"For your sake, I hope she feels the same way about you," he hissed before slamming the car door in my face.

For his sake, he should've wished that Elise hadn't felt the same way because I knew it was only a matter of time before she was going to come to my rescue and get us both out of this disastrous mess.

9

Episode 9: Law of the Land

ELISE

Pulling up to the Bernstein & Becker law firm should have been a celebratory moment. I should have been so excited to make it to the destination that I had worked so hard to get to. The last few days on the run had been so intense, and I even doubted if I'd ever be able to live a normal life again. Finally, I was in Phoenix, Arizona, and in front of the building that held the woman who was going to solve all of my problems. It should have been such a huge sigh of relief. However, Jared was supposed to be here with me. I expected the man who I began this entire journey with to be by my side in the end, and he wasn't. He was somewhere out in this world, probably scared out of his mind. Therefore, even in a moment as grand as this one, it wasn't the same without him.

Hugo had parked in front of the building a few minutes ago, but I couldn't get myself to get out of the car. I just stared out the window, longing for the man who had sacrificed himself so that I could make it here.

"Having second thoughts?" Hugo asked from the driver's seat.

"Not at all," I answered, still grateful that I was only a few steps away from this all being over. "It's just not how I imagined it."

Hugo scratched his dark beard that matched the unkempt hair that was poking out from underneath his baseball cap.

"Well, how did you picture it?" he asked. "The building looks pretty nice to me."

"Not the building," I corrected. "The feeling."

"And how did you expect to feel?" he rephrased.

"Whole ..." I uttered.

I felt every ounce of Jared's absence. I wished it would've been me who was taken into police custody, and him who had made it to his aunt's unharmed. It wasn't Hugo's fault. He was just following Jared's orders. But if I had been behind the wheel, I wouldn't have left him.

"Need some encouragement?" Hugo asked.

"Yes, please," I affirmed, still not being able to find the strength to step out of the car.

"A wise man once told me that only a fool falls in love," he began in his deep voice, "but something even more foolish than falling in love, was finding it and not cherishing it."

"What does that even mean?" I asked, baffled. For a man in his late forties, Hugo seemed to possess a lot of wisdom, but I still did not understand his riddle.

"It means get out of my car," he clarified.

At first his tone was forceful and intimidating, but then he followed up his hardened look with a surprisingly kind smile.

"Get out of my car and go finish what you started," Hugo clarified in a softer voice,

"Thanks." I smiled back, realizing it was probably time to let Hugo get back on the road. He had a mission of his own. "Same to you."

I let out one more giant sigh before finally getting out of his station wagon. Jared needed me, and it was my turn to save him. I wanted one more piece of advice before heading inside, however, Hugo drove off in a hurry as soon as I was safely out of the vehicle. I didn't blame him, though. We were both just two fools on a journey to cherish the love we had found.

Bernstein & Becker must have been doing really well for themselves because the office building stretched across the entire parking lot. There seemed to be around eleven floors that were scattered with glass windows across the exterior. I had plenty of time to imagine what the firm looked like once Jared and I eventually made it to Arizona, but it was even more luxurious than my dreams could even fathom.

I was hesitant to head inside, as I knew Jared's aunt had expressed only wanting to help him out and not me, but I managed to put one foot in front of the other until I ended up in the building's lobby. The inside was just as grand as the outside. Men in suits and women in heels populated the ground floor. It made me more aware of my own attire as my tattered beach clothes clearly did not fit in.

"Can I help you?" the young woman at the front desk called out to me. She probably also realized that I was completely out of place.

"Hi, I'm, um, looking for Laura?" I asked. "Maybe, Laura Bradley? She works in entertainment law."

I wasn't sure if Jared's aunt shared the same last name as him, so I figured it was worth mentioning what she specialized in.

"Is she expecting you?" the woman asked as she began to dial.

"Kind of," I answered. "She's expecting her nephew, Jared, but um ... he couldn't make it."

She looked at me suspiciously while the phone rang.

"Hello, Ms. Bradley," she spoke into the phone. "You have a visitor."

I anxiously waited while the receptionist alerted her of my arrival.

"No, it's just the girl," she stated. "Apparently, he couldn't make it."

I could only hear one side of the conversation, but it was obvious that Laura Bradley was asking about her nephew. I wasn't sure how she would handle knowing that he wasn't there to see her. A part of me was afraid that she was just going to send me away, as I knew she wasn't a big fan of me. However, if she wanted to help Jared, then she needed to help me, too.

After a brief conversation, the lady at the front desk hung up the phone and nodded in the direction of the elevator.

"Floor nine," she directed. "Room 912."

I wanted to leap with excitement, as I was one step closer to getting this entire mess cleaned up, but I kept a cool demeanor as I thanked the receptionist for her time. I walked the few short steps it took to reach the elevators and pressed the button. I was only a few floors away from reaching my final destination.

"One piece of advice, ma'am," the woman at the front desk blurted out just as the elevator arrived. "The next time you visit a law firm, make sure you dress appropriately."

"Thanks for the advice," I noted before stepping onto the elevator. If only she knew what whirlwind I had been through to get to Bernstein & Becker. Maybe then she would think twice about judging my attire.

When the elevator let me off on the ninth floor, I almost sprinted down the hall to find Laura's office in Room 912. However, my journey was cut short yet again by another receptionist. This time, a young gentleman greeted from behind a desk when I burst into the office space.

"I'm here to see Laura Bradley. She's already expecting me," I frantically alerted to the man, slightly annoyed at all the hoops I had to jump through just to see an attorney.

"Have a seat," he politely instructed. "She'll be out to get you shortly."

The situation I was in did not allow for any more time to be wasted by sitting around and waiting, but I did what I was told and sat in a nearby chair. While I was waiting, I tried to think of the exact words that I wanted to say to her to explain the trouble Jared and I were in, and the sense of urgency that was required in order to fix everything. Laura clearly knew the law better than I did, but she had no idea all the additional illegal things we had done along the way. Remedying the contract breaches was one thing, but getting us off on the additional crimes was another. I wasn't sure if her expertise also extended to dealing with stealing a car, sneaking onto a bus, or damaging a police car.

As more time passed, my anxiety increased and my body started to shake in the chair. I figured attorneys were busy, but I didn't think there were many entertainment law issues happening in Arizona.

"Can I get you something to drink?" the man behind the desk offered, noticing my erratic behavior. "Maybe a water?"

"I'm fine," I quickly answered, knowing that my nerves would be solved at the sight of Laura and not from quenching my thirst.

"Okay, well she should be out soon," he replied.

I stared at my surroundings, hoping that something in the office space would catch my attention and distract me from the precious minutes that were continuing to tick by. However, the paintings on the wall that depicted tropical islands only made me shudder in fear as it reminded me of the exact place I was running from.

"Someone is here to see me?" I heard an angelic voice utter from behind me.

I turned to see the most beautiful attorney I had ever seen. Her light brown hair was cut into a long bob that made her appear beyond professional. The dark gray suit that she was wearing looked like it was tailor-made just for her. Just from the sight of her, I knew I was in good hands. If her knowledge even halfway matched her appearance, the disaster I was in would be solved in no time. In fact, she may not even have to do much as I was certain that after getting one good look at her, Brent would drop any and all charges. He was a sucker for rehearsed reality television shows and beautiful women.

"Hi, Laura," I exclaimed, standing up from my chair and shaking her dainty hand.

"You must be Elise," she responded. "Jared has told me a lot about you."

I thought she would have sounded more upset to see me considering she would have rather seen her nephew, but she maintained her composure.

"I need your help," I relayed, and then corrected myself to include Jared. "We need your help."

A tiny tear escaped the corner of my eye. I had been on edge these past couple of days, and it was surreal to finally be in front of the person who was going to rescue Jared and me. It was an overwhelming feeling knowing that I wouldn't have to run away from my problems anymore.

"Let's talk in my office," she declared.

Laura led me down the hall until we reached her corner office. Honestly, I didn't expect anything less. She hadn't even helped me yet and I already knew she deserved every inch of the luxurious space.

Laura sat behind the largest desk I had ever seen and she encouraged me to take a seat across from her. Her poise and professional demeanor immediately put me at ease, even though I was constantly worried about Jared and where he was.

"I am somewhat aware of your situation from the phone calls I have received from my nephew," Laura began, "but I'd love to hear the full story from you, beginning with telling me where Jared is."

I spent some of my time in the waiting room contemplating the exact story that I was going to tell Laura, but all of that went out the window as soon as I began talking. "He's been arrested," I blurted out.

A perfectly told recollection of the previous events was not what she wanted to hear. Laura and I were on the same page about one thing, and that was saving Jared. "It took a lot for us to get to Arizona. We stole a car, snuck onto a bus, slept outside, and hitchhiked just to get here. When we crossed the state border, he damaged a police car in order to save me. I got here as soon as I could, but the police have Jared, I don't know where he is, and I am scared for him."

I admired Laura's stoic appearance, but it made it hard for me to read her. I had just explained how her beloved nephew sacrificed himself so that I could be the one to meet her, and she just continued to stare at me with the same expression she had when she first met me. Maybe it was part of her job to remain calm and act like everything was fixable when deep down she probably wanted nothing to do with me.

"Let me make a few phone calls," she uttered.

She picked her cell phone up from off of her desk and started dialing. I would have loved to witness her lawyer magic, but she left the office to take the call in private. I wasn't mad to be left sitting there, staring at the stunning views that her office provided, but I still would have rather been there to listen to the call. There could have been questions that she didn't know the answer to, or information that I hadn't explained yet. I felt like I could have been a vital piece to helping her with her investigation, but I sat back and stared at the Arizona landscape while I waited for her to return.

To pass the time, I counted the number of cars that passed by the office. It seemed to be the only thing that could possibly distract my thoughts from focusing on the dire situation at hand. I lost count several times, as I got distracted by the vehicles that cost more than the entire production budget of *Heartbreak Beach*, but on my third try, when I got to around forty-three, Laura Bradley walked back into her office.

"Well, I've got some good news and some bad news," she started. "The good news is that I know where Jared is."

A smile was begging to come out, but I suppressed it, knowing that bad news was about to follow.

"However, unfortunately, he is being transported back to California," she explained.

"That's fine, right?" I questioned. "We can just go back there and get him!"

"There's more," Laura began. "I also spoke to Brent Knox, your producer. He is willing to drop all the charges against Jared in regards to the blatant disregard for the contract that you both signed, as well as the stolen car, if you and Jared agree to finish out the filming of the finale. Apparently, he still wants you fulfill your contractual duties and film the final episode how he had originally envisioned it."

"So, if I agree to break Jared's heart on the show then we are off the hook? What about the damaged police car?" I asked.

"Jared will be off the hook," Laura clarified. "You will still be held liable for the damages caused by delaying the filming process."

"Fine, whatever," I said. "As long as Jared is free to go."

At that point, I didn't care about the show and whether it was delayed or not. I was actually proud of myself for ruining something that Brent took pride in.

"You will also claim that you coerced Jared to damage the squad car. I'll have to find another lawyer for that matter, but you will have to take responsibility for that, too," she concluded.

"So if I film the last scene, Jared is off the hook, but I'm not?" I asked. "And I have to claim that I am the one responsible for the battered car?"

"It's your freedom for his," Laura clarified. "As your attorney, I am here to advise you of your options, but as his aunt, I'm here to make sure you go back to California and give Brent what he wants."

Aunt Laura grabbed her personal belongings and started heading out of her office. I remained frozen in my chair, confused as to exactly what was happening.

"Let's go," she exclaimed when she realized I hadn't followed her. "It's time to set my nephew free."

10

Episode 10: Love is Blind

ELISE

I shouldn't have been surprised that Laura drove the entire six hours without saying a single word to me, but she managed to reach the set of *Heartbreak Beach* just as the sun was setting without even a tiny shred of conversation. I wasn't thrilled that my entire day had consisted of driving back and forth between California and Arizona, especially given the current circumstances. During the drive to Phoenix, I was worried about how Laura would manage to help Jared and me, and the entire drive back to set, I was thinking about how I'd manage to survive in a jail cell.

It was no question whether I was going to turn myself in or not and exchange my life for Jared's. To begin with, there was no way that his aunt would have let me leave her office without a fight, but above all, the love I had for Jared extended beyond the mess we were in. I would have given up myself for him, even without Laura's strong coercion. Jared had put me before himself, and now it was time for me to do the same for him.

A production assistant greeted us when we were parked in the same lot that Jared and I had initially begun our journey in—where we stole Victoria's pink Mini Cooper. Funny enough, the police had managed to bring it back to her as it was parked only a few spots away from us. We were only able to drive her car to a town a couple of hours away before we left it at the sketchy motel, so it didn't surprise me that it was able to make its way back to the lot so quickly. Victoria probably didn't even notice it was gone unless she took inventory of the wigs that she kept in her backseat and noticed that two of them were missing. We may have left them in the duffel bag by the campsite, so I was hoping she wasn't expecting them back.

"Right this way," the production assistant instructed as he led us to set.

Laura and I were both eager for the filming of the finale, although for different reasons. She just wanted her nephew to be exonerated of his crimes, and I was looking forward to being reunited with the man who had not only stolen a pink car, but my heart.

We approached the beach, in the same spot where I had been initially instructed to deny Jared's request of leaving the show with him. It was a weird feeling, as it almost felt as though the whole escape had never even happened as I was still dressed in the same clothes, the camera crew was in their same positions, and the sun was setting similarly to when the scene was originally filmed. I was only missing my co-star, who was currently being dragged back to set with a police officer on each side of him with Brent leading the way.

"Elise, get out of here!" I heard Jared scream. "It's not worth it!"

He struggled against the officers' grip as they dragged him across the sand.

"Elise," Brent greeted when he was standing in front of me. "Funny to see you here."

I rolled my eyes at his sarcastic comment and set my sights on Jared.

"And you must be Jared's aunt," Brent uttered, shaking her hand.

"Laura Bradley," she introduced firmly. "I'm representing my nephew, Jared Bradley. I want to proceed with the filming of the final episode so that I can bring my client back home."

"Pushy," Brent said with a smirk. "I like it."

I knew he would be enamored with Laura's beauty. I was hoping it would distract him enough to just let both of us go free, but that was a request not even Laura could make happen.

"Well, let's get to it then. Places, everyone!" Brent shouted as he and Laura retreated behind the cameras. As soon as the accompanying officers let Jared go and joined them, Jared and I ran to each other in pure desperation. When our bodies came together, my heart immediately felt full.

"Elise, you can't be here," Jared whispered into my ear as he hugged me tightly.

"I had no other choice," I replied. "The only way to save you was to come here—my freedom for yours."

Jared kissed me as if it was the last time he would be able to. The passion behind it made my stomach flutter, and it even further solidified that I was making the right decision.

"Leave the beach with me," Jared remarked. "Let's leave the same way we came ... together."

My heart ached, as that was not the plan. If I wanted Jared to go free, I had to dump him.

"Jared, I can't," I explained as tears were streaming down my face. "That's not part of the deal."

"Forget the deal," Jared said. "We will face whatever comes our way, together. You and me, Elise. Leave the beach with me, please."

I stared into his eyes, confused as to how I was even supposed to find the strength to break his heart. He had been by my side the entire time, and his only wish was to go through everything together. Jared didn't want to be saved—he wanted to be loved.

"Okay," I whispered against his mouth, giving in to his request. "I'll leave *Heartbreak Beach* with you."

Jared pulled me in for a kiss again, making the first one seem like a small peck. His desire for me was felt through every second of the kiss, and his hand around my waist held on to me for dear life. Another tear escaped from the corner of my eye, but this time it was because of my feelings for Jared and the love that we shared.

"And scene! Great work!" Brent Knox shouted. "That's a wrap ladies and gentlemen. *Heartbreak Beach,* season one, is now complete."

After Brent made his announcement, Jared immediately pulled away from me and wiped the saliva off his mouth as the rest of the crew clapped.

"Can I get a towel?" he called out. "And maybe a water?"

An eager assistant ran to Jared's rescue with a white rag in one hand and a bottle of water in the other.

"Thanks," he replied as he unscrewed the cap and took a large swig.

Members of the crew began to pack up the camera equipment, and one even raced over to Jared to remove his mic.

"Um, am I missing something?" I questioned, wondering why everyone was celebrating the finale that did not go the way that Brent had instructed. "What's going on?"

"The most epic season finale in reality television history," Brent chimed in as he walked over to us. "That's what is going on."

"Excuse me?" I asked. It appeared as though Brent was actually pleased with how the ending turned out, which confused me even more. I tried to look at Jared for comfort, but he didn't seem baffled by the situation at all.

"What?" Brent started. "You didn't think that Jared came up with the escape plan all on his own, did you?"

Brent turned toward Jared who was dabbing his face with a towel.

"No offense," Brent said.

Jared just shrugged off the comment and took another sip of water.

"Can someone please explain to me what is going on?" I cried out.

Everyone just seemed to carry on with the deconstruction of the set, not even caring that I had no idea what was happening.

"The whole escape was carefully orchestrated and secretly filmed," Brent revealed. "None of it was real."

Brent was one of the most evil human beings I had ever met, but there was no way everything I had just gone through was scripted.

"That can't be true," I stammered. "I was the one who left the set in the middle of the scene. I was the one who ran back to my trailer and started this all."

"We were going to pause the scene and call for a five-minute break anyway, but you ended up doing that part for us," Brent noted. "It was actually perfect timing."

I stood there frozen, not believing a thing Brent was saying. I replayed all the moments in my head, trying to think back to a point in our escape plan that couldn't have been rehearsed.

"What about Victoria's car?" I pointed out.

"It was purposely left unlocked," Brent stated. "The money, the wigs in the backseat—it was all planted there."

"What about the cops? What about Aunt Laura?" I questioned, gesturing toward the woman who I thought was the lawyer I had traveled hundreds of miles for.

"All actors," Brent relayed.

My mind was racing a million miles a second, trying to comprehend what had just happened.

"I don't get this. I don't get any of it!" I cried out. "So everything I just went through was fake? Your actual plan for the final episode was to take me on a wild goose chase?"

"I knew you weren't heartless enough to actually dump Jared, and I knew you would agree to run away with him," Brent explained. "The viewers are going to enjoy seeing how you both will go to the ends of the earth just to be together—a true testament of love. I will say, though, I did underestimate your feelings for him, but it made the scenes more believable."

I thought I was the puppet in this master plan, but Jared was really the one under Brent's control. Brent had somehow managed to convince him to go along with his stupid idea.

"What was even the point?" I raged. "Ratings? Viewership?"

"Not just that," Brent responded. "I wouldn't have dragged you through everything just for some high markings and a couple of views."

"Then, why did you?" I pleaded.

"Longevity," he answered with a giant grin.

"Longevity?" I questioned.

"This finale will go down in history as one of the most iconic endings to ever air on television. Your future is set. Your career is set. *Heartbreak Beach* is going to put us all on the map," Brent announced with pride.

I turned to Jared who was happily standing by the smug producer's side.

"And you're okay with this?" I fired at him.

"I mean, it did make for a good finale," he uttered.

The man who I thought I was sacrificing my freedom for suddenly turned into someone I didn't recognize. The sweet, caring side of him was no longer visible, and all that was left over was pride and ego. He didn't care about me—he never cared about me. All of this was just some ploy to solidify his career on television, but it came at the expense of my emotions. I should have never trusted him.

I was still trying to process the last few minutes. I couldn't decide whether I wanted to scream, cry, or attempt to break every camera in sight, but I did know I couldn't stand to look into the eyes of the man who had betrayed me and the producer who had plotted the entire thing. I abruptly turned away from them and simply began to walk away, trying to distance myself as far away from the set as possible. There were no words left to say to either of them. They didn't deserve another second of my time.

"We'll have a car take you to the airport!" Brent shouted after me, pretending to be concerned.

I had no idea where I was going or what I was doing. All I knew was that I couldn't be on that beach any longer. I continued to trudge through the heavy sand, just trying to get as far away from them as possible. I just wanted to be left alone and be given the proper space to wrap my head around the humiliation that I just went through, however, I heard someone briskly run up next to me. I looked up and saw Jared standing in front of me.

"Hey, Elise. One last thing before you go," Jared said to me, holding my hand and staring deep into my eyes. "Thanks for not breaking my heart on national television."

I ripped my hand away from his and continued to trudge along the sand. I should've known this was all fake. His acting skills were the only thing more pathetic than his desire of being on TV.

11

Episode 11: Heartbreak Beach

JARED

"Can you chew any louder?" I asked my brother as he began munching on the pizza he had bought before getting on the plane. It was a long flight from Los Angeles back home to Boston, and I didn't want to listen to him eat the entire time.

"Sorry," Marshall mumbled with pizza in his mouth. "I worked up an appetite being a television star."

"You were only in a few scenes," I argued back.

"So?" he defended. "It still made me hungry."

Marshall pulled out his phone, and was rewatching the unedited content that Brent had sent us. The finale hadn't aired yet, but we still wanted to get a sneak peek.

"Why'd you choose the name Abraham, anyway?" I asked, watching the clips with him. "You could've picked anything else."

Marshall swallowed the chunk of pizza that he had just bitten off.

"I don't know. You chose George Washington," he reasoned. "I thought we were doing a U.S. presidents theme."

I rolled my eyes at my brother's lack of creativity, but I guess I couldn't blame him for coming up with a name on the spot. Neither of us were expecting Elise to ask for his name. However, that wasn't the only thing that happened unexpectedly. Although the entire chain of events was carefully thought out by Brent, some things didn't go as planned. The main one being that I jumped in front of the wrong car to hitchhike from. That may have been my fault as I was told the exact make and model of the vehicle that the hired actor was in, but it was hard to tell what kind of car was approaching from where we were standing on the side of the road. Thankfully, Hugo was still nice enough to give us a ride and not run me over, but it definitely made the plan a lot harder to execute. When I used Hugo's phone to call Brent and alert him of the little hiccup, he was understandably upset as the car we were in didn't have the hidden cameras. That part of the show might have to be heavily edited or portrayed from the perspective of the camera crew's car that was following closely behind us—at least I still had my mic on. The worst part was that I had to basically beg Hugo to pull into the correct rest stop where I knew our fake police officers would arrive at. It would have ruined the entire finale if he had chosen another gas station, but thanks to my amazing acting skills, I was able to get him to stop.

"Would you like some peanuts or pretzels?" the flight attendant asked Marshall and I when she reached our seats.

"Me and my television star brother will take some pretzels," he answered.

I rolled my eyes as the fame was already getting to his head, and the finale hadn't even aired yet.

"Maybe you can be my co-star one day," he said to her. "Your face was made to be shared with the world."

The stewardess handed us each a small bag of pretzels, unaffected by Marshall's claim of being an actor, and his pathetic attempt at flirting. She probably realized that if we were actually rich and famous celebrities we would have been sitting in first class.

"Is it my lucky day or are all flight attendants as pretty as you?" he flirted.

"Must just be your lucky day," she unenthusiastically answered.

My brother pulled out a pen from his backpack and signed the napkin that she had given him with the bag of pretzels.

"For you, sweetheart," he replied, handing it to her. "Remember the name, Marshall Bradley, better known as, Abraham, the hot motel receptionist."

She reluctantly took the napkin from him which I was very confident would soon end up in a trash can.

"Seriously?" I asked him when she walked away.

"What?" he responded. "You're not the only one who can pretend to fall for a girl."

He opened the bag of pretzels and began popping them into his mouth while he continued to watch the unedited clips.

"Oh, that's the best part right there," I commented, as the scene of me ripping my shirt off and punching the breakaway glass windshield of the squad car was playing on his phone.

"You think you would hit the gym more if you knew your stomach was going to be broadcast to the entire world," he muttered.

I ripped the bag of pretzels from his hand and ate one out of spite.

"I look good without a shirt," I said, patting my stomach.

"Yeah, sure," Marshall sarcastically noted, putting his phone away and stealing back his pretzel bag. "Do you think Elise ever caught on?"

I thought back to the adventure we had gone on together and tried to think of a time where there was almost a slip up.

"Maybe when we camped out in the woods," I answered.

I had slept in the trailer Brent had prepared for me about a few yards away. The production crew members who were camping out with me were supposed to wake me up before Elise noticed I was missing, but they had fallen asleep. That was an easy mistake to cover up, but I wasn't expecting the jelly on the knife in the duffel bag. Our props guy was notorious for snacking on jelly-filled doughnuts. Apparently, he had used the prop knife to cut into one of them and got the blade all sticky. I didn't know if Elise had noticed or not, but I was fully prepared to act like it was blood if she had asked. I did not want her inquiring any further about it, so I figured telling her it was blood would have scared her off from asking any more questions. It was already convenient enough that there was a bag of camping supplies perfectly placed in the woods near our campsite. I didn't want her suspicions to get raised any higher.

"There should've been a part in the script where Abraham and Aunt Laura got together and fell in love," Marshall remarked.

"I don't think the motel receptionist and the entertainment lawyer getting into a relationship is realistic," I argued while grabbing on to the armrest as the little bit of turbulence caught me off guard.

"Yeah, well, neither is you pretending to faint and sneaking onto a bus to Las Vegas," he fired back.

Marshall had a point, but I didn't know what he expected. Brent was a producer for reality television shows, not for chart-topping action movies. Despite the poor idea, it was executed to perfection, if I must say. I passed out like a pro, and even though everyone in line for the bus was a paid actor, I still sold my performance.

"You think there will be a season two?" my brother asked.

"Even if there is one, there's no way it's going top this season," I replied.

I was a little biased, as I would always favor the season of *Heartbreak Beach* that I was in, but I was sure that Brent Knox had plenty more tricks up his sleeve.

"Maybe you two will stage a breakup, and then Elise will be the star of the next one," Marshall suggested.

"I doubt she ever wants to be on television again," I explained.

Our contract had a clause in regards to appearances and interviews that we were obligated to take part in after the show aired, but Elise had probably gotten herself a good lawyer by now and would most likely fight the rest of the stipulations in the agreement. She probably didn't want to see me ever again, but I doubted her attorney would be able to get her out of everything. I was sure there would be a time when we would have to reunite, forced to sell the idea that we were in love. I'd always wondered what it would be like to be in a fake celebrity relationship, and who better to be in one with than the girl who I punched a fake cop car for.

I'd be lying if I said I wasn't excited to see Elise again sometime in the future. Though my love for her was only for the cameras, a small part of me felt bad for her. It was sad to see her fall for me when I knew it was all fake. However, at the same time, she should have been more aware. I mean, I didn't know how she didn't see it coming. Granted, the big reveal in the end when we explained to her that everything was scripted—the part where she actually got her heart crushed—wasn't going to air, she still got heartbroken ... on a beach ... it's literally in the name of the show.

I reclined my seat and put on my headphones to try and drown out the sound of Marshall's chewing.

"Oh well," I said to myself, "I guess not everyone can find true love on a reality television show."

A Note From The Author

Thank you for reading my novella, *Heartbreak Beach*. Make sure you follow my social media accounts and subscribe to my newsletter for information about upcoming releases. My self-publishing journey would not be able to continue without you, so I appreciate your amazing support!

Subscribe to my newsletter:
https://linktr.ee/authorbaileythomas